Georgie couldn't even look in Pierre's direction, because the minute she did, she knew that she would have a vision of him alongside that big king-size bed in his bedroom.

Pierre swung her around to face him and his face was like granite.

"Don't even think of doing the maidenly outrage act, Georgie!" His voice was soft and silky, and as cutting as a whip. "Are you suddenly finding the consequences of your actions a little too uncomfortable for your liking...?"

Georgie looked at him mutinously and found herself being distracted by his eyes. Amazing eyes, and fabulously long, thick, dark eyelashes... She blinked and forced herself back to the reality of him gripping her shoulders.

"And don't even think about getting into your shell of a car and trying to drive back to your cottage in this weather."

"I wasn't," she said. "But if you were any kind of gentleman, you would offer to drive me. *Your* car could handle the trip easily."

Pierre answered without batting an eyelid.

"But I'm no gentleman."

CATHY WILLIAMS was born in the West Indies and has been writing Harlequin® romances for some fifteen years. She is a great believer in the power of perseverance as she had never written anything before (apart from school essays a lifetime ago!). From the starting point of zero has now fulfilled her ambition to pursue this most enjoyable of careers. She would encourage any would-be writer to have faith and go for it!

She lives in the beautiful Warwickshire countryside with her husband and three children, Charlotte, Olivia and Emma. When not writing she is hard-pressed to find a moment's free time in between the millions of household chores, not to mention being a one-woman taxi service for her daughters' never-ending social lives.

She derives inspiration from the hot, lazy, tropical island of Trinidad (where she was born), from the peaceful countryside of middle England and, of course, from her many friends, who are a rich source of plots and are particularly garrulous when it comes to describing Harlequin Presents heroes. It would seem from their complaints that tall, dark and charismatic men are way too few and far between! Her hope is to continue writing romance fiction and providing those eternal tales of love for which, she feels, we all strive.

BEDDED AT THE BILLIONAIRE'S CONVENIENCE

CATHY WILLIAMS

~ SNOW, SATIN AND SEDUCTION ~

TORONTO • NEW YORK • LONDON
AMSTERDAM • PARIS • SYDNEY • HAMBURG
STOCKHOLM • ATHENS • TOKYO • MILAN • MADRID
PRAGUE • WARSAW • BUDAPEST • AUCKLAND

Recycling programs
for this product may
not exist in your area.

ISBN-13: 978-0-373-52744-1

BEDDED AT THE BILLIONAIRE'S CONVENIENCE

First North American Publication 2009.

Copyright © 2008 by Cathy Williams.

www.eHarlequin.com

Printed in U.S.A.

BEDDED AT THE BILLIONAIRE'S CONVENIENCE

four hours ago a miserable sandwich she had grabbed at the

CHAPTER ONE

GEORGIE eyed the glass building staring her in the face and decided right there and then that this was positively the very last time she would let herself be guided by impulse. Even if the impulse had its roots in all the right reasons.

The only halfway decent part of her tortuous trip from Devon had been the taxi ride from the station and even that had ended on a sour note with an *unnecessarily* disgruntled taxi driver dumping her outside the security barrier, not paying a scrap of attention to her very reasonable plea that he hang on *just a few minutes* in case her party wasn't inside.

Now she had no idea how she was going to run the wretched man down to ground. The building looked as though it was riddled with security guards and CCTV cameras, all aimed at making sure unwanted riff-raff didn't intrude their ridiculously overpriced premises.

As if anyone in their right mind would actually *want* to invade *a gym*. Most of the people she knew spent the majority of the time working out how they could *avoid* one.

Plus it was cold.

Plus the last time she had eaten had been approximately four hours ago, a miserable sandwich she had grabbed on the hop, and her stomach was making all those churning noises that suggested it needed feeding and quickly.

She took a deep breath and breezed up to the revolving doors. At seven fifteen the place seemed to be populated by men. Short ones, tall ones, fat ones and, needless to say, none of them her quarry.

There was a huddle of young, fit people behind the circular reception desk, guarding the turnstile gates like Rottweilers, Georgie thought unpleasantly, and she approached them with care.

Despite the fact that they didn't seem to be doing anything at all urgent, it was still a few seconds before one of them, a young girl with very blonde hair pulled back into a high pony-tail and sporting the look of a highly trained cheerleader, arched one eyebrow and asked if she could be of service.

The look on her face as she gave Georgie the once over suggested that her finger was probably on the Emergency button even as she asked the question.

'I…yes, I hope so…' *I am a fully trained primary school teacher*, Georgie thought, *and a pipsqueak of a girl in a tight Lycra outfit isn't going to intimidate me!* 'Actually…I…'

'Are you here to enquire about joining? If so, I can tell you straight away that our books are completely full for the next eight months.'

'No, actually, I'm not here to join…'

The arched eyebrow rose fractionally higher. 'Then?'

'I'm looking for someone…one of your members, actually…'

The blonde exhaled one long, impatient sigh and glanced at her watch. 'I'm afraid I won't be able to help you with that. Our members come here to relax in very exclusive surroundings. The last thing they need is to be pestered by people they may not want to see. I'm going to have to ask you to leave.'

She swung her head around to her supervisor, who was an older version of her, and Georgie realised that she was now probably going to be accosted by the full pack of Rottweilers.

'I'm afraid I must insist on being allowed in to find Mr Newman,' Georgie addressed the older thirty-something blonde, fishing out her best teacher voice, the one that implied dark and dastardly punishment if her orders weren't obeyed immediately. It never failed to work on her four year old protégés and, sure enough, the older woman stiffened slightly.

Georgie realised that it wasn't the voice, more the *name* that had generated this reaction.

'Would you mean *Mr Pierre Christophe* Newman?'

'I'm surprised you can recall his name off hand considering your club is *so oversubscribed*,' Georgie couldn't resist saying. Really, she wasn't surprised at all. Pierre Christophe was not the sort of man people usually overlooked. Well, not unless you had pretty much grown up with him. Then, she thought loftily, his impact wasn't quite the same!

The older blonde woman seemed suddenly flustered but still she managed to drag her sales patter out of the hat, informing Georgie that Highview wasn't oversubscribed, that they merely maintained a firm control over the number of members, as exclusivity was what they aimed for. 'Some of our members are extremely important and extremely wealthy individuals,' she elaborated smugly. 'We aim to make sure that they can come here knowing that they can relax away from their busy schedules. The gym facilities are never overcrowded, nor is the pool and all the other things we have on offer. We prefer, in fact, to think of here more as a very exclusive retreat than anything else!'

Georgie politely listened and thought that it sounded very boring indeed. Lots of over pampered millionaires taking time out from ordinary people, as if they were incapable of relaxing unless surrounded by people who were of the same social standing.

Pierre would fit in just nicely, Georgie thought. She could distinctly remember him as someone who accepted other people's subservience as his right and had successfully built a life of such staggering wealth that he need never venture out of his cocoon unless he wanted to. He snapped his fingers and they came a-running. A far cry from Didi, which reminded her why she had come to London in the first place and she held up her hand, putting a halt to the sales diatribe.

'That's great, but I'm not interested in joining. I'm here because I need to see Pierre as a matter of urgency. If you point me in the right direction, I'll find him myself, or else I don't mind waiting if you want to search him out.'

'It's not our custom to allow non-members into Highview's exclusive fitness area.'

'Fine. I'll stay here. You can tell him that Georgie… *Georgina* needs to have a word with him.'

'May I ask what it is about?'

'You may, but I'm afraid I won't be telling you. It's of a *personal* nature.' She tried not to laugh as the woman frantically tried to control her curiosity. Poor Pierre wouldn't be too happy to think that people might be speculating about some unknown tawdry secret about his private life behind his back, but then he never had had a sense of humour. At least, not one that he had ever pulled out of the hat for her benefit.

No, Georgie's memories of him were that he was exceptionally good-looking, already a young man when she was still experimenting with lipstick and padded bras, with a talent for disapproval. He had disapproved of pretty much everything there was to disapprove of in their small village in Devon and he had never attempted to hide it.

He had disapproved of what he considered a way of life that

was so slow it bordered on static, disapproved of his parents and what he considered their hippie lifestyle, disapproved of anyone, it had seemed to her, who didn't share his own burning ambition to leave his home town as quickly as he could so that he could make his mark in the City. And since he had hit London well over ten years ago, his return trips to Devon had become more and more infrequent and far between.

He had returned for his father's funeral three years ago and, although he had spent a fortnight making sure that his mother was all right, handling the sale of the farm with a disconcerting lack of sentiment considering he had spent nearly half his life growing up on it, buying a more suitable cottage for her closer to the centre of the village from which she could walk to the shops, Georgie had had the distinct impression that he had been itching to wrap up the whole business and clear off back to London as quickly as he could.

Since then he had been to see his mother a handful of times. If the truth be known over the past few years, Georgie had made sure to keep out of his way whenever he was around.

Which made her, yet again, curse herself for her tendency to jump right into things, both feet first, eyes closed, fingers crossed.

The blonde was telling her that she would get someone to find Mr Newman and repeating how terribly inconvenient it all was and, of course, should he not wish to see her, then she would be escorted off the premises immediately. Company policy.

Georgie struggled to remember that the woman was probably just doing her job.

While she waited patiently on one of the red, low chairs that were artfully arranged around a chrome table on which several company magazines promoted the wonders of the gym, she took time out to survey her surroundings.

This was obviously the holding area for the unprivileged

few not allowed behind the magic turnstile. Perhaps delivery men. Beyond the turnstile and behind the reception desk was a marble foyer, from which stairs led up to presumably the gym area, which was behind smoked glass, and straight on was a marbled corridor leading to goodness only knew what. Swimming pools and squash courts, she suspected and possibly some exclusive beauty parlour where businessmen could have their tension knots kneaded away by some more of the blonde clones.

She surfaced to find Pierre standing right in front of her, a towel draped round his shoulders, feet planted very squarely on the ground.

Georgie's eyes travelled up the length of his body until she finally met his eyes. Blue, blue eyes from his father and, from his Algerian mother, the swarthy colouring and raven black hair, cut short and at the moment still damp, leading her to think that she must have interrupted a swimming jag.

He was frowning. 'What are you doing here, Georgina? Clarice told me that you needed to talk to me urgently. Is something wrong with my mother?' The frown deepened. 'I spoke to her on the weekend and she seemed all right. Well, don't just sit there like a stuffed doll! What the hell's going on?'

Having kept out of his way the last few times he had travelled down to Devon, Georgie had forgotten just how intimidating Pierre was up close and personal.

For starters, he was tall, over six feet and every inch of his body exuded menace, from the hard, muscular body to the imperious beauty of his face.

Yet he was a sensationally attractive male, blessed with perfect bone structure and the sort of *presence* that made women spin round in their tracks to get a second look.

Georgie considered herself immune to all that raw, sensual appeal, however. For her, the blue eyes were icy cold and the wide, sexy mouth carried an underlying cruelty that was like a forcefield around him.

'There's no need to shout, Pierre.'

'I wasn't shouting. I was asking a perfectly civilised question.' He gripped both ends of the towel and eyed her with barely concealed impatience. Yet another one of his off putting character traits, Georgie thought. 'I don't often find time to relax and the last thing I need is to have my routine interrupted by someone playing hard to get. If you have something to tell me, then spit it out.'

Georgie sprang to her feet and glared back up at him. 'Well, nothing ever changes, does it, Pierre? You're still the *rudest* man I have *ever* met in my entire life!'

'So tell me something I don't already know. If I recall, you've shared that opinion with me on several occasions in the past, the last time memorably being when I came to Devon for my father's funeral! While everyone else were paying their respects, you were busy letting me know what an inconsiderate human being I was! Not that any of that matters. Just tell me what you've come to say.'

'Look, I don't want to argue with you. Didi's fine. Ish.'

'Ish? What the hell does *that* mean?'

'Is there somewhere we could go and…talk? I know I'm dragging you away from the joys of working out, but I *have* come all the way from Devon…' Uninvited, unannounced and ill prepared, but, heck, he wasn't to know that. 'I've had a hellish time of it, in case you're interested. Delays at Plymouth, vile sandwich on the train, signal failures everywhere, surly taxi driver…not to mention using up endless credit on my mobile phone trying to get your secretary to tell me where you were! It was worse than pulling teeth! Tell me, has she ever tried out for a job in the secret service?'

'Natalie knows that when I go to the gym, I don't like to

be disturbed.' But he relaxed slightly. Maybe he had been a little harsh on her, but for some reason the woman had always rubbed him up the wrong way. Everything about her irritated him, from her glaring, judgemental moral high ground to her annoying tendency to say just whatever happened to pass through her head, without any vetting process. He liked his women perfectly groomed and perfectly in control. Opinions were welcome provided they were thoughtfully considered and open to healthy debate. Pierre, in fact, considered himself an eminently twenty-first-century man who enjoyed the company of highly intellectual women and supported their right in the workplace. Georgie was at the opposite end of the scale when it came to the attractions of the opposite sex and ten minutes in her company was usually enough for him.

'I gather,' she was telling him now. 'She made it abundantly clear in the twenty minutes it took to wrench the information out of her.'

'What did you tell her?'

'That I was the woman you secretly married on the weekend and I threw in Didi's name to give my story a bit of authority.' Course, she hadn't, but it was worth the little white lie to see the expression on his face. 'Just kidding.'

'Hilarious. There's a café in the gym. We can go and talk there.' He spun round on his heel and began walking away while Georgie glowered at his departing back.

Needless to say, with Pierre preceding her, she was whisked through the forbidden gates like visiting royalty. The man, wherever he happened to go, had clout. He walked and doors opened. Any wonder he was so infuriatingly superior?

'I'm shocked they let me through,' Georgie said breathlessly, trying to keep pace with him and look around her at the same time. 'They're not a very welcoming bunch out there. Do they get special training in how to be impolite?' she wondered aloud.

'Most of the members here lead highly stressed lives.' Pierre slowed down and looked at her unruly blonde head. 'This is their sanctuary. The last thing they need are people turning up unexpectedly because they need to discuss a work-related matter.'

'And would you say that's a frequent occurrence? Something that warrants an army of blonde clones baring their teeth at anyone they don't recognise?'

'You'd be surprised,' Pierre murmured, omitting to mention that she would probably have received less short shrift if she hadn't been wearing an assortment of clothes that frankly bordered on the eccentric. Odd-looking flat suede boots that were thickly fur lined, thick black tights, a black poncho type coat and something very red beneath it, heaven only knew what.

They had reached the café and Georgie paused to take it in. There were cafés and then there were, obviously, cafés for the super rich in private elitist surroundings. Certainly the café at the local gym near her, which she had been to all of three times, was a lively, usually packed, 'queue up for your mug of coffee or bottle' of water type affair. This was in a different league altogether.

'I don't think I've ever seen so much black leather outside a furniture shop,' she announced, openly staring. There were only a handful of people in the vast sitting area and all of them were reading newspapers.

'What do you want to drink? Tea? Coffee?'

'Tea, I guess.'

'Only healthy stuff here, I have to warn you. So think fruit teas or Darjeeling.'

A few minutes later and Georgie was sitting in front of a cup of aromatic tea, which, she suspected, would taste like dishwater.

'Right. Now are you going to tell me the purpose of your visit here, Georgie? What did you mean that my mother is well-ish? If there's any health problem at all, then I don't intend to sit here and play guessing games with you about it.' Pierre sipped some of his coffee and looked at her coolly over the rim of his cup.

Now she was divested of her artistic poncho, he could see that the glimpse of red was, in fact, a brightly patterned jumper of which red was but one of the primary colours.

'Has someone gone mad with a paintbrush on your jumper?' he found himself asking, and Georgie beamed and looked proudly down at herself.

'As a matter of fact, several little people went completely mad with paintbrushes and this is the result. Christmas present from the class last year. If you look closely you'll see that the splashes are, in fact, four-year-old renditions of themselves all overlapping one another and everyone's written their name under their pictures. Adorable, isn't it?'

Pierre grunted. 'Unusual. You were telling me about my mother.'

'She's fine.' Georgie tried some of the tea but after one sip she hurriedly returned the cup to its saucer.

This, strangely enough considering she had known Pierre for so many years, was the first time she was actually having a one to one conversation with him in private. Usually, on the occasions they had met in the past, they had been surrounded by mutual friends, family and acquaintances, and over the past few years even those accidental meetings had petered out. Once his father had died, Didi had lost interest in the big parties they had become famed for throwing.

Now Georgie was noticing things about him that had not been apparent. He was as arrogant as she remembered, naturally, but there was also a watchfulness about him, as if nothing, not one little stray word or movement, was going unnoticed. It made her nervous and she had to stop herself from fiddling with her cup or playing with her hair.

It was obvious from his silence that he was waiting for her to carry on. Silence, she imagined, was a quality he would have found useful.

'After that minor stroke she had earlier in the year…Didi's just not been the same.'

Pierre frowned. 'The consultant informed me that she would make a full recovery and I needn't remind you that he was the top guy in his field.'

'She *has* made a full recovery…'

'Then where are we going with this?' Pierre glanced at his watch. As always he was running on a very tight schedule. He still had some important emails to send off the minute he returned to his apartment and tonight he was seeing Jennifer. After a fortnight of trying to work around their packed agendas, they had finally managed to fix up a dinner date in between their work commitments.

'Sorry, am I keeping you from something?' Georgie enquired coldly.

'I might have been able to spare you more time, Georgie, if you had given me some advance notice… Believe it or not, I lead a pretty busy life here.'

'And I *would* have done, but I came here on impulse.'

'Typical.'

'What does that mean?'

Pierre looked at her, taking in the unruly blonde hair, the bizarre clothing, the huge green eyes, which were more often than not narrowed at him in judgement. 'I have no idea how you manage to hold down a proper job, Georgie.'

'And I have no idea how you ever manage to have fun, Pierre.'

'There you go again. Talking without thinking.'

'You feel free to make comments about me. Why shouldn't

I return the favour?' Georgie felt her hackles rise. Predictably. Didn't they always when she was in his presence? 'Because I'm impulsive doesn't mean that I'm irresponsible!'

'How are the chickens, Georgie?'

She glared at him. Yes, she kept chickens. Just four of them. They clucked around happily in her back garden and laid a steady supply of the best eggs anyone could hope for. Pierre, naturally, was mystified by that small gesture of animal husbandry. In a minute he would doubtless mention her sprawling vegetable patch where she grew everything from carrots to runner beans. He had only ever been to her house once, on an errand from his mother, but it had been enough to cement in his mind a completely distorted picture of her as a slightly batty young woman totally out of tune with the twenty-first century.

'The chickens are well and fine, Pierre.'

'And the self-sufficient lifestyle?'

'*You* are infuriating!'

'I know. You've told me.' Pierre grinned. He had to admit that she *did* do maidenly outrage very well indeed. All flushed cheeks and flashing eyes.

'It's common sense,' Georgie said through gritted teeth, 'to have as organic a lifestyle as possible—'

'Oh, spare me. I spent years listening to that claptrap from my parents. I don't need to revisit that tired old place again.'

'There's nothing wrong with growing as much of your own food as you can. At least when I pull up my vegetables, I know that they haven't been doing freestyle in a swimming pool of fertilisers!' She looked around her with scathing condescension. 'I don't know how you could do all this, Pierre.'

'All *what*?' His voice was very quiet, which made her think that it might be an idea to abandon the developing conversation.

'All *this*. The clinical expensive gym, the clinical expensive apartment in the heart of the city. I mean, *you grew up on a farm*!'

'Correction. I grew up in a boarding school. I had holidays on a farm and that was enough for me to realise that as permanent lifestyles went, it wasn't one I cared to pursue. But you didn't come here to catch up, did you, Georgie? You might be impulsive but you're not *that* impulsive.'

'It's a little awkward…'

Pierre recognised the sheepish tilt of her head, the way her eyes shifted away from him, her body language as she drew back slightly. *A little awkward.* Could only mean one thing, really. She needed money for something and she had come to beg. Only somewhere along the line she had forgotten that beggars should be humble and accommodating.

A humble Georgie. Should make interesting viewing, he thought. He decided to watch her wriggle in her own discomfort and inclined his head to one side with an expression of lively but uncomprehending interest.

'I mean…'

He leaned forward and frowned helpfully.

Georgie sighed dramatically. 'This tea's awful. Have you ever tried a fruit infusion? Disgusting. I don't suppose you could get me a coffee, could you? I'd love a latte, as a matter of fact. Haven't had one of those for ages…'

Pierre could recognise delaying tactics from a mile away. He forgot about the important emails waiting to be sent and nodded. 'Sure.'

'I know you're probably in a rush…'

'Take your time, Georgie.' He flashed her a smile and wondered how she would ask the favour she had clearly come to ask. Georgie was as proud as they came. Must be something very important that would have her come to him cap in hand. 'I'll go get you that latte and maybe something to eat? They do a nice line in bran muffins and fruit and nut bars. Should be right up your street.'

'Because I have a vegetable plot doesn't mean that I *like* bran muffins and fruit bars!' She watched as he stood up, fishing in the pocket of his jogging bottoms for his wallet. He absolutely towered. It wasn't simply his height, but all that impacted muscle on show. His arms were lean, brown and hard and his torso had athleticism and grace. She couldn't actually remember noticing all this about him, but then again she had rarely spent time with him on a one-to-one basis and certainly never here, in London, on his turf. The saying 'Lord of all he surveys' sprang into her head.

He returned moments later with a latte for her and some mineral water for himself which he drank straight from the bottle.

'So…' he leaned forward, his hands loosely linked between his legs '…why don't you ditch the pleasantries, Georgie and cut to the chase?'

'Ah.'

Pierre sighed impatiently. The emails could happily wait for a couple of hours, allowing him to savour the rare opportunity of watching her squirm, but Jennifer, his carefully arranged date, could not. He decided to speed things along a bit and help her out of her obvious misery.

'You haven't travelled all the way from Devon to give me a hard time about my choice of lifestyle. And you've told me that my mother is fine—'

'Ish.'

'Fine…fine-*ish*. At any rate if there was anything wrong I would know about it by now. Which just leaves us with one possible reason why you might have undertaken a four-hour trip to spring a visit…'

'It does?'

'Money.' Pierre sat back, sipped some of his water and continued to watch her. 'Makes the world go round,' he said lazily, 'or not, in some cases. So how have you managed to get into debt, Georgie?' He played over a few scenarios in his head. 'I thought a teacher's salary in Devon could go a pretty long way. Not much there to spend the pennies on, after all…'

Georgie momentarily found herself distracted and bristled at his criticism. 'No clubs like this, at any rate, Pierre. But I wouldn't say you *spent* money in a place like this. More *wasted* it! Anyway, I haven't come here to—'

He held up one imperious hand. '…argue with me. Yes, yes, yes. I understand that, although I notice that you just can't seem to help yourself. It's that bossy boots disposition of yours, Georgie. If you don't watch it, you'll end up organising the local Women's Institute…and don't burst a blood vessel just because I happen to be telling you the truth. I mean, you can't even keep that tongue of yours under check when you've come here to ask a favour from me! Because you have, haven't you? Come to ask me a favour…'

Technically speaking, Georgie supposed that that was true-ish and, while she briefly pondered how he had managed to shove her into the role of beggar *when she wasn't*, she caught him smiling smugly at her and shaking his head.

Unfortunately, while she wanted to jump in and vigorously set him straight, actually telling him why she had madly hopped on a train to London was beginning to present itself to her in all its dubious glory. She would just have to let him ramble on for a bit while she tried to rationalise what she wanted to say and work out how she had managed to forget just how *objectionable* the man was.

'Okay. Spit it out. Where has your money gone?' Pierre raised his eyebrows in a question. Close up she could see that those blue eyes which she had always imagined to be as cold as the winter sea, could also darken when he was amused, as he now evidently was at her expense. 'House extension for a few more animals?'

He appeared to be giving the conundrum a great deal of thought. 'Luxurious chicken coop because they deserve the best? No? Well, I can't imagine you having expensive taste in clothes and jewellery...' He looked her up and down and Georgie scowled back at him in return. That was one thing he had always been very good at. Making her feel gauche and unappealing when it came to her choice of clothing. She had never had conventional taste when it came to what she wore, and over the years she had come to recognise that expression in those blue, blue eyes when he looked at her as a sort of vague, unspecified contempt.

But then the man lacked imagination. She only had to think of the women he had brought back to his parents; house over the years. Humourless intellectuals who had been fine rabbiting on about world affairs, economics and the British legal system but at a loss discussing anything else.

'It's not practical wearing designer suits to teach kids,' Georgie felt compelled to defend herself.

'Did I imply that it was?'

'You didn't have to.'

'So it's not the clothes because, as you pointed out, you don't see the point of wearing anything expensive or feminine—'

'I never said that!'

'If you're not in long gypsy style-skirts, you're wearing jeans, Georgie. I think there's a distinct possibility that you emerged from the womb clad in various layers of flowered fabric. So we've established that it's not excessive retail therapy. Hmm.' He watched her splutter with a feeling of satisfaction. Hard to occupy the moral high ground when your secret vices had caught you out!

'Having fun, Pierre?'

'Always amusing to watch the preachers come undone...'

'I am not a preacher!'

'No? I remember a number of tedious sermons on my appalling personality, my ruinous obsession with money, my lack of proper filial concern…the list goes on.'

Georgie reddened. Put like that, it *did* make her out to be something of an interfering, prissy bore, and for the first time it was driven home just how much of a pain he had always seen her. Too close for comfort and hence too familiar for the subservience he enjoyed. In a world where wealth and status were everything, he was the undisputed king of the city. The way he was treated at the over priced gym in which they were now sitting told its own story of deference and respect. She, on the other hand, had always been the burr under his skin and still was.

She wondered whether it would be possible to abandon her cause and slink off back to Devon without explanation.

'So tell me why you want the money. It's been fun imagining the possibilities but the game has reached its limit. I need to be out of here and I dare say you need to head back to Devon.' He had momentarily forgotten about Jennifer, but a quick glance at his watch told him that he would have to get a move on.

He looked at her impatiently and realised, with surprise, that she seemed stuck for words.

'Oh, for God's sake, Georgie. Just spit it out. I haven't got time for this.'

'I don't want to borrow money from you, Pierre. I haven't run myself into debt gambling on the internet, or…or anything else! I've come to tell you that…that…' her mind went a complete blank and she licked her lips nervously '…you and I are…well, it's kind of difficult to say this…but…we're—'

'Oh, for God's sake. *What?*'

'Engaged! Or as good as…'

CHAPTER TWO

'What!'

Pierre's thunderous bellow had several heads swinging interestedly in their direction. Georgie didn't think that too much bellowing took place in the hallowed confines of the gym café. Did extremely rich, extremely influential people *bellow*? Probably not. However, this one did.

'Explain yourself!' Pierre commanded, leaning forward in his chair and thereby sending her nervous system into frenzied overdrive.

She cleared her throat and tried to maintain eye contact. 'There's no need to get into such a state about it…'

'No need to get into such a state…? What planet are you on, Georgie? You hustle up to London uninvited, accost me at my gym and then calmly inform me that *we're engaged*…and I'm not supposed to be just a little bit taken aback?'

'Practically engaged…well, more sort of *seriously* involved…'

'You've finally lost the plot, Georgie. You need to be on medication. Either that or making best friends with your local shrink.'

'Look…I know we've had our differences over the years—'

'That's the understatement of the century!'

'But just hear me out.'

'I'm all ears.'

'As you know, I'm very close to your mum… I try and look in on her practically every day. Just to make sure that she's all right.'

'And she is.'

'In a manner of speaking.'

'Look, you're trying my patience here. I don't have the time to play word games. She's fully recovered after her stroke. I spoke to her consultant myself, and believe it or not, I do telephone her once a week.'

'But you don't see her.'

'Let's not go down this road, Georgie,' Pierre said tightly. 'It's a little too well travelled for my liking.' He was finding it difficult to rein in his anger and stupefaction at what she was saying. Having been born into a life of relative ease, the recipient of a family fortune that had descended through the generations, Pierre had single handedly seen his parents fritter it all away on a series of ill-thought-out-and bizarre schemes, from organic farming when organic had been barely a word in the dictionary, to investments in companies that had sunk without trace the minute his father had flung money at them.

It had never seemed to unduly bother either of his parents but it had bothered him.

Consequently, he had, from an early age, determined that the fate of his parents would never be his. He would make his fortune and he would exercise relentless control over both it and the course of his life.

He had remorselessly stuck to his game plan, and by the time his father died and the true extent of his debts were revealed Pierre had already amassed several fortunes and was considered one of the greatest financial talents in the country. His discipline was legendary.

Naturally not in Devon where he and his mother maintained an uneasy but superficially smooth relationship. He visited her when his hectic schedule allowed and paid lip-service to his duties as a son.

But, hell, had she *once* ever congratulated him on his achievements? Even when he had paid off every penny of debt incurred by his father? And installed her in a cottage, of her choosing, with an allowance that wildly surpassed what she could possibly hope to spend in a lifetime?

Of course not.

Still. He couldn't believe what he was now hearing. Seriously involved with this crazy blonde? A teeth-grindingly irritating woman whose greatest talent was rubbing him up the wrong way?

'I'm not going to humour you by listening to this nonsense.'

'Pierre, Didi's really depressed.'

'Everyone gets depressed from time to time,' he snapped impatiently. 'It's rarely a matter for concern.'

'Didi isn't the sort of person who gets depressed.' Lord knew why she had bothered with this idea, which had seemed so good at the time but which, now, in the face of Pierre's icy scrutiny, was fast beginning to appear ill conceived and frankly insane. 'Yes, she's recovered and her health should be good, but over the past few months she's stopped doing all the stuff she usually does. She no longer goes to her bridge club twice a week. To start with, she told me that she physically wasn't up to it, but I began to worry when she stopped altogether. Then, she's given away her ducks to the children's farm—'

'And about time too.'

'She's had them for four years, Pierre!' She was leaning forward, trying to impart some of her urgency, although she didn't seem to be making much headway. 'She still does some of her charity work but several times this month I've been to see her in the morning before I head out to school and she's still been in bed—'

'What time do you head out to school?'

'Eight-fifteen.'

'I rest my case. My mother is no longer a spring chicken. Maybe she just feels that at her age she deserves the occasional lie-in.'

'It's not like her.'

'People change when they get older,' Pierre said shortly.

'I know you've probably got lots of important things to do, Pierre, but I've come here from home to talk to you and I'm not going to leave until you've heard me out.'

'I might be mistaken, but isn't it my *choice* as to whether I listen to what you have to say? And as far as I'm concerned, I've frankly heard enough.'

'I wouldn't be here if it didn't concern your own mother. Do you think being shouted at and insulted is my dream way of passing the time?'

She wondered what she would do if he decided to just get up and leave. Run after him tugging at his shirt sleeves and scrabbling in his wake? Anyone would think that he would *want* to hear what she had to say, but then again he had never had the same level of love and affection for his own flesh and blood as she had had for them.

Their parents had been great friends and when both of hers had died in a car accident when she was still a teenager, Pierre's parents had taken her under their wing and virtually adopted her as their own. Pierre, at that point, was already beginning his meteoric rise through the world of serious finance and she had, she suspected, filled his vacant shoes. Not that she hadn't been close to them before, and not that they had loved him any the less, but he just hadn't been around.

If he had resented that then he certainly hadn't shown it. He had visited and treated her with the condescending politeness of someone who considered himself out of her league.

Pierre shook his head and stood up and Georgie could see her most dire imaginary scenarios of shirt-sleeve clutching begin to take shape but actually he just said, abruptly, 'I have to be somewhere tonight so if you want to talk, and believe me I'm only doing this through some semblance of politeness, you're going to have to come with me to my flat and talk while I get dressed. It's the best I can offer.' He didn't wait for her to reply but instead picked up his sports bag and began heading for the exit with Georgie trailing frustratedly in his wake.

Normally he got his driver to take him to the gym, but on this occasion he had driven himself, and his Bentley, gleaming and black, was waiting in the car park.

Georgie bit back the temptation to say something flippant about how the other half lived. Somehow she suspected that any jokey remarks would go down like the proverbial lead balloon.

But it didn't seem quite right to talk about anything serious while he was concentrating on driving through London. In fact, it barely seemed comfortable to talk at all, and she was quite happy to stare out of the window and watch the streets of London crawl by.

The few times she glanced over to him, she felt her heart begin to pound harder in her chest. His profile, perfectly etched, was grimly forbidding. No wonder people quailed in his presence, she thought. He had probably specialised in fear induction at university, along with economics, law and politics.

His house was in Chelsea and Georgie, who knew absolutely nothing of London, could tell at a glance that it would have carried an almighty price tag. Maybe it was the rarity of the square around which fanned out the crescent of tall, red bricked Victorian buildings, each identical with their impeccable façades, their little steps leading up to front doors and their ornate black railings. Despite being in the very heart of fashionable London, the area still managed to exude quiet, secluded privacy.

Or maybe it was the tell-tale display of expensive cars parked outside.

'It's lovely here, Pierre,' Georgie said, to break the silence which was beginning to stretch like elastic between them. 'Very quiet…in fact, does anyone actually occupy these houses? I see cars and a few lights behind windows, but where *is* everyone?' She laughed nervously as he opened the front door.

'This isn't a small village in Devon, Georgie.' Pierre turned to her briefly. 'Neighbours don't waste hours chatting over the garden fence.'

'You'd be surprised what a person can find out over a garden fence.'

'Really? Not much of interest to me, I don't think.'

'Well no, I guess not. I mean, we don't make idle chat about the stock market or the latest takeover bids in the private sector.' The last time Georgie had met one of Pierre's girlfriends, she had been subjected to a long and sleep inducing conversation about the wonders of the New York stock exchange, where, apparently, the woman had worked for three years before returning to London to head the futures department of an investment bank. Georgie could remember nodding a lot but really just wanting to chew her own arm off in boredom and frustration at the other woman's patronising attitude.

'No.' Pierre pushed open the front door and preceded her into his hallway. 'Why break out of the mould when it's so much easier to just pass the time of day talking about local gossip and the farming industry?'

'Why are you so…so…*arrogant*, Pierre?'

He tossed his keys on the small console table in the hall and ignored her. 'Close the door behind you, Georgie. I've just about got time to offer you a cup of coffee, or something stronger if you want, although, if I recall, you prefer to keep clear of that evil stuff. Then I'm going to have to change.' He glanced over his shoulder with a small frown. 'Where do you intend to stay tonight?'

Georgie was busy having a thorough look at his house, or at least what she could see of it. It wasn't quite what she had expected. She had expected something cold and minimalist, a bit like the man himself, but it was a surprisingly warm place. The entrance hall was tiled, but the colours were strong and earthy, reds and terracottas and blues and creams. There were paintings on the wall, recognisable rural scenes, and the banister leading up to the first floor was gleaming oak.

'Well?' he demanded and she reluctantly tore her inquisitive eyes away from the rest of her surroundings.

'I didn't really think about it.' Georgie shrugged. 'Actually, I thought I might have arrived in London a lot earlier, but there were delays at every stage. Still. I guess I could travel back tonight or else maybe you could point me in the direction of a cheap and cheerful bed and breakfast? If you know where one might exist?'

Pierre leaned against the doorframe and looked at her through narrowed eyes but he didn't say anything. Instead, he turned on his heel and disappeared through the doorway so that Georgie was obliged to follow him, though very slowly because she had no intention of rushing her inspection of his house.

There were two rooms on either side of the generous hall and she could make out cool creams in one and in the other what appeared to be a fully operational office, complete with all the gadgetry of the twenty-first century, although the walls were lined with books and the Oriental carpet extending across most of the floor lent it an intimate, cosy atmosphere.

'In your own time!'

Pierre's voice interrupted her inspection and she guiltily looked up to find him back in the doorway waiting for her.

'Sorry.'

'Really? Somehow I find that a little hard to believe.' And this time he waited for her, stepping aside so that she could precede him three steps down into a dining area and then beyond that into the kitchen which was big enough to house a table along with all the usual culinary paraphernalia.

'You notice that I didn't mention anything about that nonsense you were spouting in the café…' he turned to her, a mug in his hand '…because I wanted to give you time to consider very carefully what an impossibly stupid idea it was. I also didn't want you to somehow get it into your head that I would take it seriously *on any level whatsoever,* because I won't. However…' he filled the kettle and switched it on '…if you tell me that my mother is acting out of character, then I need to know about it, even if I don't necessarily agree with what you're saying. So…' he dragged one of the chairs from under the table and sat down, hooking his foot under another, which he proceeded to use as a footrest '…I'm listening. Make the most of it.'

'You mean my time starts now?'

'You said it.' Pierre folded his arms and gave her the benefit of his undivided attention.

'This wasn't how I envisaged having this conversation,' Georgie said, heading for the kettle because it was obvious that he had given up on the coffee-making idea. Sure enough she didn't see him rushing over to relieve her of the task of making her own drink. She opened her mouth to ask him where she could locate the coffee and heard herself ask him whether she could pour herself a glass of wine.

Pierre's eyebrows shot up in surprise. 'Dutch courage, Georgie?'

'What do you expect? You haven't exactly been welcoming.'

'What did you think I would do?' He stood up, strolled over to the matt silver fridge and pulled out a bottle of Chablis, then poured them both a glass. 'Hear you out and then jump up and down with glee at your hare brained scheme?'

'Well, hearing me out would have been a start.' The wine was delicious, very cold and very dry, and Georgie took a long mouthful before looking at him.

'So I'm hearing you out now. You tell me my mother isn't herself. Well, why don't you let me decide that for myself?'

'You mean you'll visit her?'

'I mean I'll give her a call and ask her what this is all about.'

'And suddenly she'll pour her heart out to you! Down the end of a telephone!'

'Why not?'

'Because that's not how people work, Pierre! Least of all your mother. You know how proud she is and also…'

'Also?'

'She's in awe of you.'

Pierre flushed darkly at what seemed to be a criticism thinly disguised as a compliment of sorts. He drank the contents of his wine glass in one long mouthful and frowned. 'Explain.'

'I mean she would probably hate for you to think that she was being weak.'

'This conversation is going nowhere and I have to get changed.'

Georgie hastily drank her wine, determined to finish what she had travelled hours to say even if he intended on being stunningly unhelpful. He gave no indication that he was aware of her following him although when she paused at the doorway to his bedroom, he said, without bothering to turn around, 'Not going to advance any further, Georgie?'

Georgie opened her mouth and then, like a stranded goldfish, gulped noiselessly as he began to strip off, starting with his sweatshirt, which he pulled over his head in one smooth gesture. He still hadn't turned in her direction and she stared with crawling fascination at the beautiful muscularity of his body. He was a physically perfect specimen, with the golden olive complexion inherited from his mother.

When he finally did turn round, their eyes collided and Georgie looked away quickly, her face bright red. She went even redder as he hooked his fingers under the waistband of his jogging bottoms and tugged them lightly.

'You're welcome to look if you want to,' he said and she made a strangled sound, which finally evolved into something coherent.

'Perhaps I should wait until you're finished having your shower.'

'Feel free, but I'll be on my way out and, unless you want to accompany me on a date, then I suggest you get on with saying what you want to say here.'

'I…I wouldn't want to *embarrass* you…'

'You mean you wouldn't want to embarrass *yourself*.' Pierre laughed and stripped off his bottoms. 'Believe me, I don't embarrass easily and certainly not when it comes to getting undressed in front of a woman. That's the joys of being brought up in a boarding school. You lose hang-ups about nudity pretty quickly.' But it still felt as if he were performing a striptease, although her face was pointedly averted and her hands were fisted at her sides.

He went into the shower, turned it on and kept the door open, pretty much expecting her to scuttle off the minute his back was turned, but instead when she spoke he discovered that she had pulled the dressing-table chair by the door and, although she couldn't see what he was doing, she would certainly be able to hear well enough.

Her prudishness amused and surprised him at the same time. The woman was in her twenties! He wondered, for the first time, what sexual experience she had. Any? In her own way, she was quirkily pretty and there must be one or two eligible men in the village, fellow teachers on the lookout for suitable wife material…

'I finally had a chat with your mother a couple of days ago!' Georgie had to all but shout to drown out the sound of the shower. 'I asked her about the bridge business and she finally came out with it…'

'Came out with *what*?' Pierre turned off the shower and stepped outside, wrapping a towel round his waist and proceeding to fill the sink with warm water for a shave.

Now she could see him. Or at least the back of him. When he looked in the mirror, he could actually meet her eyes.

'Ever since she had that minor stroke, she's been depressed. She said that it started off with not really being interested in anything, then she began finding it too much of a bother to get out of bed. Sometimes she would just stay put until lunchtime, and then she would only get out because she knew that there was a chance that I would pop in later in the afternoon on my way home from school.'

'She never mentioned a word of any of this to me.' Pierre paused and looked at her in the mirror. 'No, don't tell me. It's because she's scared of me.' He was very still but he could feel the little tic in his jaw.

'Of course she's not scared of you!' Georgie wondered whether her voice sounded a little brittle. Didi would never have been critical of her son behind his back, but it was so easy to read between the lines. Pierre and his mother did not enjoy a comfortable relationship and over the years she had accepted the blame for that, much to Georgie's dismay. She blamed herself for sending him to boarding school because Charlie had boarded, as had his father and his father before him, because it had been the tradition. Then she blamed herself for not living up to what he had wanted, for being selfish and pursuing an eccentric lifestyle which she and Charlie had loved but which had mortified and appalled their son. She was ridiculously proud of him but whenever he was around she felt as though she were walking on egg-shells and that, she confessed, had probably put him off wanting to return to Devon to visit as often as she would have liked.

And then there was the matter of the women he had brought to meet her.

'Although,' Georgie was compelled to admit, 'you *can* be a little off-putting.'

Pierre dropped the razor and washed his face without bothering to shave at all. He strolled out of the bathroom and towered over her, arms folded, his mouth drawn into a thin line.

'Meaning?'

'You have a very abrupt way of dealing with people.'

'I'm not woolly-headed, if that's what you mean. I realise my mother might rather I ended up running a holistic centre on a farm somewhere in Devon, but she just has to accept that that will never happen.'

'Don't be silly.' Georgie stared at his stomach, which was very flat and very hard. The top of that towel was slung rather low round his waist for comfort. Her eyes skittered upwards. 'But she's getting older. I *think*…no, I know that her depression is tied in with the fact that she thinks she's lost you. Lost you to London and big business.'

'London and big business are what made sure that my father's debts could be settled and a place bought for my mother—'

'Yes, I know that, but…'

'But what?'

'Didi's in a slump,' Georgie said flatly. 'I went to see Dr Thompson a few days ago about it and he was quite frank with me. He said that she's at an age where psychologically she could literally *think* herself into an early grave. Apparently it happens particularly to people left on their own after their partners have died. They become depressed and over time it eats away at them until they literally lose the will to live. He's against giving her antidepressants because he says that they can become addictive and end up being as much of a problem as the original depression, and Didi is totally against taking them.' She had his full attention. He raked his fingers through his hair and walked across to the huge, deep chair by the window, which he proceeded to swivel in her direction so that he could continue looking at her.

'He told me that the best tonic for Didi would be for her to have something to look forward to, something that might help her make sense of her days—'

'She could have whatever she wanted,' Pierre interrupted brusquely. 'I have always made it perfectly clear to Didi that money was no object when it came to her wants or needs. If she wants to go on a cruise, then she just has to say the word. That would make a nice change. Older people favour cruises.'

'Didi? *A cruise*?'

'Maybe not a cruise,' Pierre said quickly, thinking of his unorthodox mother to whom a cruise of any sort might well be construed as some form of punishment.

'What Didi wants is something that can't be bought. I managed to drag it out of her in bits and pieces and she's told me that the only thing she really wants is for you to be happy, for the both of you to have some sort of rapprochement…'

'There's nothing wrong with our relationship.' Pierre stood up, went across to his wardrobe and yanked open the door. Quite frankly, the thought of sitting over an elaborate French dinner with Jennifer didn't seem very appealing at the moment. Three hours ago his life had been a calm, ordered affair, just the way he liked it. Not so now.

'I never said there was,' Georgie was quick to reply. 'I'm just trying to explain *more fully* why I came here…your mother would like to see you settled. I think, in some weird way, she feels responsible for the fact that you've never married… I think she feels that your background was unstable and now you're reaping the dividends of something that she created without ever meaning to—'

'What a load of rubbish.' Out came his boxers, which he slung on, then a pair of black trousers. 'I don't believe in all this psychobabble. I suppose you encouraged her into *letting it all hang out?* I suppose you persuaded her *to open up?*' He shot her an acid look. 'You might teach little kiddies on how to do finger-painting and simple sums, but that doesn't give you insight into other people's lives!'

'I know it doesn't!'

'Then what did you think you were playing at encouraging my mother to try and analyse herself? She seemed perfectly all right the last time I spoke to her a week ago!'

'Well, she wasn't and she hasn't been *all right* for a while!'

'And your solution, having sat her down on a couch somewhere and imparted your amateur pearls of wisdom, was to tell her what? That she needn't worry any more about her wayward son because, lo and behold, he was, in fact, going out with *you!* Never mind that I have a perfectly well-balanced emotional life. In case you'd forgotten, Didi has actually met a few of my past girlfriends.'

'Um.'

'*Um*? What does *um* mean?' He was barely aware of pulling a shirt out of the wardrobe and putting it on.

'Nothing.'

'You've come this far, Georgie! Don't tell me that you're going to dry up on me all of a sudden!'

Looking at him, Georgie actually *did* feel as though her mouth were suddenly stuffed with cotton wool. Her thought processes, for a few confusing seconds, also seemed to be malfunctioning.

He looked terrifyingly good-looking. He hadn't bothered to brush his hair, but simply swept it back with his fingers, and there was a rakish, piratical look about him that was at odds with the formal wear. When she had been a silly teenager, she could remember looking at Pierre from the sidelines and feeling a frisson of sexual awareness. Retrospectively, she had put that down to a teenage crush, one of those endearing 'ogle from a distance' kind of things that every girl had and eventually outgrew.

Right now, the frisson that rippled through her felt disturbingly similar and she had to drag herself back to the reality of who he was and why she so heartily disapproved of him.

'Okay. By *um* I mean that your girlfriends…well, they aren't exactly *easy company*, are they?'

'I've never had a problem.'

'Because you enjoy discussing world affairs and fiscal policies.'

'You mean the boring stuff that makes the world go round?'

Georgie drew in a deep breath and ploughed on. 'I mean your mother has always found your girlfriends a little difficult to warm to…'

'I'm finding it difficult to believe that Didi's sunk into a depression because she hasn't warmed to my past girlfriends. Which reminds me…' He looked at his watch and, with a sinking heart, Georgie realised that she had made her convoluted journey and got precisely nowhere, which now left her the awkward task of gently hinting to Didi that the unlikely romance with her son was at an end, or else carrying on with the charade but with the absence of the leading man. Neither was a particularly palatable option.

With stunning accuracy, Pierre looked at her narrowly and pointed out that, aside from anything else, what she had plotted in that scatterbrained head of hers amounted to little more than deception.

'And you know what they say about those webs of lies…' he rounded off, before slinging on his jacket and leaving the room.

'I was desperate!' She found herself tugging at his jacket and yanked her hand back as though it had been burnt. But the ruse worked because he did, at least, turn to look at her.

'I'll say this for you, Georgie. You're persistent. If you could just harness that persistence to, say…something boring like an interest in world affairs, then who knows how far you could go?' He would never admit it but her remark about his girlfriends had hit home and he fully believed her when she told him that Didi found them difficult companions. Like Georgie, his mother was a 'live each day as it comes' fellow bohemian to whom the gravitas of anything serious was to be sidestepped.

'And anyway,' he continued, resuming his sprint downstairs, 'what would you have told her when the whole phony relationship had come to its natural conclusion?'

'Oh, who knows, Pierre? Maybe I could just have shunted you off to the New World and created a whole alternative lifestyle for you! Perhaps explorer? Missionary? I could have transformed you into something other than a money-making machine and also done you the favour of relieving you of any responsibility to ever visit your mother again!'

That stopped him in his tracks and when he turned to face her his expression was hard. 'Be careful, Georgina. I allow you leeway in view of our history, but there's only so far that I'm prepared to go. Shooting your mouth off about matters of which you are ignorant is unacceptable. I enjoy seeing my mother. If I don't get to see her as often as we would both like, then that's to do with the lifestyle I lead. Companies don't magically run themselves. They need someone at the helm and that someone happens to be me. And before you launch into another speech about the pointlessness of being a *money-making machine*, just cast your mind back to where my family fortune went and the debts my father accumulated leading his carefree, relaxed existence.'

'He was happy! They both were!'

Pierre sighed. 'I know that, Georgie. Look, I have to go. You'd better sleep here tonight. It's too late for you to head back home and I won't let you out to roam the streets in search of a cheap place to stay. There are towels in one of the closets upstairs and you can take your pick of either guest room. There's also food in the kitchen. You can work your way around. Television's in the downstairs sitting room.'

'Who are you going out with?'

Pierre raised his eyebrows in dry amusement. 'Is that a leading question?'

'I don't know what you mean.'

'I *mean* that if I tell you that her name is Jennifer Street and that she's a corporate lawyer specialising in tax, will the information be duly noted and used at a later date in evidence against me?'

Georgie grinned reluctantly. 'I admit it might be,' she confessed.

'So, then, I'd better say that her name's Candy Floss and she's a stripper at a nightclub…'

'Some things are just a little too hard to swallow, Pierre, and that's one of them!'

'Because the only thing I really know how to do is make money and the only women I would consider dating are women who make money as well? We don't just talk about world affairs, Georgie,' he said softly. 'We also have fun…'

For a few seconds, Georgie felt as though the oxygen had been sucked out of her. A vision of Pierre and his corporate lawyer *having fun and not talking about world affairs* jostled for position in her head and as she met his eyes, saw the lingering smile on his mouth, she was struck by his raw sexuality in a way she never had been before.

'Well, please give my proposition some thought, Pierre…' She struck out for some neutral territory to banish her wayward thoughts, although her voice sounded nervous and high-pitched. 'I'm really concerned…' *Drop it by a couple of decibels*, she thought. 'I'm really concerned about your mother and I would do anything to get her out of her state of mind, even if it means carrying through with a pretence. I'm not your type…' she thought of his elegant, tax-lawyer-style girlfriends having fun before repairing somewhere for a civilised discussion about stock markets '…any more than you are mine…but your mother would be happy and that might be all it would need to give her the strength to get her life back on track…'

Why the hell was he feeling guilty? Pierre had no idea because there was no part of him that felt responsible for his mother's state of mind. He was a dutiful son and, yes, perhaps he could visit with more regularity, but how many times had he invited her to London? To stay with him? Time and again she had refused. No, he had met Didi more than halfway. Yet…

'I'll see you tomorrow, Georgie,' he said abruptly. 'Turn the lights off when you head upstairs.'

He left with his conscience annoyingly murky, which did

nothing to advance the enjoyment of his evening. Worse, he began to wonder whether Jennifer really *was* a touch on the dull side and found himself mentally counting the number of times she referred to her work.

Which meant that he returned to the house much earlier than he had expected. Too early for Georgie to be in bed, judging from the lights shining in the hall. As he walked into the house he startled her emerging from the sitting room, washed and make-up-free and wearing one of his tee shirts and some old jogging bottoms, which she had belted with one of his ties.

They stared at each other, she in surprise at his early return and he in reluctant admiration for an outfit that looked sexy without trying, and just then the telephone rang…right there on the table next to her… What could be more natural than she should pick it up…?

CHAPTER THREE

OR RATHER, what could be more natural to Georgie? The phone rang, she automatically reached for it. She even did it in her friends' houses and could only explain it away as a habit formed from spending so much time in a school where taking calls was not delegated to anyone in particular but to everyone in general.

Pierre, in the act of removing his jacket, could tell immediately that she knew the caller. Her face broke into an easy smile, the sort of smile that would, without much provocation, he thought, be accompanied by the sort of infectious laugh that would always make even the most dour bore grin. In fact, thinking about it, that laugh had lodged somewhere in his head because he knew exactly how it would sound.

She placed her hand over the receiver and mouthed, *It's Didi*. Divested of his jacket, Pierre frowned and began loosening his tie, then he held out his hand for the phone. His opening words were, as Georgie turned away allowing him privacy for the call, 'Didi. What are you doing calling at this hour? Is something the matter?'

Then she headed for the kitchen because somehow it felt awkward to be retiring to bed knowing that he was prowling downstairs. Fine if she had been asleep when he had sauntered back, but now she felt obscurely obliged to stay up until she made sure that she formally told him goodnight.

Belatedly, she realised that she had kitted herself out in some of his clothes, but they *had* been hanging in the spare wardrobe, which sort of implied that they weren't used, and she *hadn't* had the foresight to bring spare clothing because she had jauntily expected to be making the trip in one day. Wildly optimistic in retrospect, which was something else to be said for avoiding too much impulsive behaviour.

Anyway, she wondered, what was he doing back so early? It wasn't yet eleven! She made herself a cup of coffee and mentally smirked at the notion that his idea of *having fun* couldn't involve too much of a courtship routine if he could wrap the entire evening up in under three hours! Perhaps tax lawyers preferred speed over romance!

It was beautifully warm in the kitchen. Beyond the kitchen table was a small area with two squashy sofas and a television, which was where Georgie now removed herself with her mug of coffee, and she was beginning to feel quite drowsy when she heard him enter, although she didn't turn to face him.

Instead, he was virtually upon her before she noticed his thunderous expression.

'Okay, okay!' Georgie sat up and made a conciliatory gesture with one hand. 'I *know* I shouldn't have borrowed your clothes but they were doing nothing in the wardrobe in the spare room so I just assumed they were surplus to requirements. Maybe just in a holding bay before being shipped off to the nearest charity shop.' He still looked like a volcano on the verge of erupting, which, to her, seemed a bit of an overreaction to her using some of his spare clothes. 'I'll take them off if you really feel *that* strongly about the whole thing.'

'I don't give a damn about the clothes, Georgie!' He completed the unfinished task of stripping off his tie, which he proceeded to hurl on one of the chairs.

'Oh, that's a relief,' she said uncertainly. 'Course, I'll take them back with me and return them to you dry-cleaned.'

'I said *I don't care about the clothes*!'

From the tone of his voice, Georgie seriously didn't want to explore what precisely *was* concerning him, so she looked at him in mute silence. 'Can I make you a cup of coffee…or something?' she asked eventually.

'Coffee?' Pierre went to the fridge and spoke grimly into it. 'I think I need something a lot stronger than a cup of coffee!' Which involved a generous amount of whisky, some soda and ice, which cleverly popped out of a dispenser in the freezer door.

At which point he sat on the sofa next to her and gave her a long look that was only marginally warmer than the ice in his glass.

'Is a habit of yours to answer other people's phone calls?' he opened.

Georgie felt the jaws of a trap yawn open under her feet, but she greeted this remark with an apologetic smile. 'I know. It's awful. An awful habit. It's because there's no receptionist at our school. At least there hasn't been one for ages. The last girl left and since then we've spent our budget on more important things, which means that the phone calls come directly through to the staff room and it's up to whoever's in there to field the calls. So when I hear a phone ring, I just tend to pick it up without thinking.'

'Which pretty much describes how you do most things, Georgie. *Without thinking. Without thinking* you fabricate some ridiculous story about the two of us having a relationship…*without thinking* you hare up to London to try and suck me into your crazy scheme…*without thinking* you grab the telephone the minute it rings without any notion *whatsoever* for respecting someone else's privacy—'

'I admit my common sense sometimes lags behind a bit—'

'*Sometimes?*' He swigged a mouthful of his whisky and soda and looked at her acidly. 'Well, the outcome of your common sense *lagging a little bit behind* is that my mother is now convinced that that little fairy tale you spun for her is one hundred per cent true. Why else would you be answering my telephone at ten-thirty at night if we weren't involved in some heady relationship? Seems you told her that we'd been meeting up now and again over time but you didn't want to say anything to her because, apparently, it was all too new? I'm not sure when these so-called meetings were supposed to take place, but no doubt you have the answer to that mystery!'

'Some weekends,' Georgie admitted in a small voice. She stared down into her cup of coffee and prayed that the ground might open and swallow her up, possibly flinging her back in time to before she had recklessly opened her big mouth and dug herself into a hole.

'Some weekends…' Pierre repeated flatly and she nodded.

'I airbrushed over the details,' she mumbled. 'Just sort of implied that it had been all very clandestine and exciting. I know I shouldn't have done it but your mother was crying a bit, saying how much she wished that you and her were closer, that she would die without ever seeing any grandchildren born, that she didn't understand those women you had brought to see her in the past…'

'And, finding your tender heartstrings tugged, you decided that the kindest thing you could do would be to concoct a fantasy about us!' He didn't much care for the thought of his mother crying. She wasn't a crier. In fact, he remembered her as being full of life, laughing a lot, drawing people around her because of her exuberant personality. She hadn't been born in England but she had married his father and however much he had disapproved of their irresponsible lifestyle, he had to admit that she had integrated perfectly into the country life. Had, in fact, become something of a pillar of society.

'I'm not a monster,' he told her briefly. 'I can see you might have been tempted to soothe my mother, but she's fallen for your story hook, line and sinker.' He sat back and momentarily closed his eyes.

'She must have been very upset when you told her the truth,' Georgie said quietly. 'You have every right to be annoyed…'

'Annoyed?' He opened his eyes and stared at her incredulously. '*Annoyed?* Annoyed is something you feel when you're waiting for a letter and the postman arrives an hour late! Annoyed is not being able to find where you've left your house keys!'

'Oh, all right,' Georgie snapped, 'I get the picture. *Enraged*, then. Is that a better word?'

Pierre looked at her narrowly. 'Why do you imagine I would rescue you from the discomfort of letting Didi down yourself? After all, *you're* the one who got us both into this mess in the first place.'

'You mean you didn't say anything to her?'

'She wasn't in the frame of mind to have her high hopes dashed.' He had finished his drink and he now stood up, but, instead of refilling his glass, he poured himself some water and sat back down on the sofa. It gave her barely any time to consider her options. Or rather to face her one and only option, which would be to slink back down to Devon and confess all. She was pretty sure that whoever composed the motto about confession being good for the soul hadn't been thinking of this particular scenario.

'What frame of mind was that?' Georgie asked weakly. Like a moth drawn to an open flame, she felt compelled to learn all the details that would make what she had to do all the more painful.

'Happy? Optimistic? Girlishly excited? Are you getting the picture here?'

'Loud and clear,' she said gloomily. 'Don't worry. I'll explain everything to her tomorrow. Didi will understand. In fact, she'll probably be touched that I cared enough to think about embarking on such a crazy charade.' Either that or she would be bitterly disappointed, but Georgie wasn't going to contemplate that outcome.

Pierre cursed under his breath and sprang to his feet. 'How the hell could you put me in this position?' He began pacing the kitchen, pausing now and again to glower at some innocuous gadget before transferring his attention back to her.

'I'm sorry. How many more times do you want me to say that? Maybe you want me to write it out a hundred times as punishment?' Georgie stood up. 'I should be getting off to bed now. Tomorrow looks like it's going to be a marathon day.'

'Sit back down!'

'What for?' She placed her hands squarely on her hips and glared at him. For once she wished that she were a strapping Amazon of a woman, someone who could look at him on eye level and impart some authority, instead of a slip of a girl, five feet four and boyishly built. He absolutely towered over her, both physically and mentally.

'This conversation isn't over!'

'Well, I don't see where else it can go, Pierre! I messed up. You've told me that I've messed up. I shall have to go and clean up the mess I made. How much more simple can it get?'

'I went along with the pretence,' he said darkly, and Georgie looked at him in startled disbelief. Her mouth fell open.

She sat back down and watched as he dragged a stool over

and swung it round so that he could sit on it, resting his arms on the wooden, slatted back.

'Why?' she asked faintly. 'You spent the past few hours listing all the reasons why you refused to have anything to do with my plan…why on earth would you change your mind at the last minute?'

'For a start, I wasn't allowed to draw breath. I haven't heard my mother that animated since…my father was alive.' He ran his fingers through his hair, a restless gesture of baffled frustration. 'You must have done a damned convincing job on blurring over the edges of your little piece of fiction. Didi was thrillingly convinced that we truly *had* been conducting a secret affair, although I can't understand how she could have been so easily taken in. When did she think we had been meeting up? Did it not occur to her that she would have seen considerably more of me over the past few months if I had been pursuing you?'

Georgie was still grappling with the fact that he was prepared to go along with her idea. Now, of course, she was beginning to have second thoughts.

She hadn't remembered him having such a powerful effect on her. How was she supposed to be conducting a relationship with a man who could knock what remained of her common sense from her in the space of five seconds? Would it be possible to mention his name to Didi with a dreamy look in her eyes when her teeth were grinding together in frustration at his overbearing, arrogant personality?

'Did you put that to her?' Georgie asked and Pierre shook his head dazedly.

'I intended to,' he admitted, 'but it was a bit like being in the path of a bulldozer.'

'So what happens from here?' Georgie was entertaining the idea that they could conduct this mysterious yet impassioned affair without actually ever being seen in the same place at the same time. It would be a lot easier to look dreamy eyed about him if he weren't physically around, getting under her skin.

'I guess,' she said, staring off into the distance and thinking aloud, 'I could chat about you with Didi, giggle over a few girlish tales, disappear on the occasional weekend… I know it sounds deceitful…'

'Don't get me wrong, Georgie. I still don't approve of what you did and it *is* deceitful. On every level. You made me an accomplice to your scheme—'

'I wish you wouldn't call it a *scheme*.'

'Too close to the knuckle for your liking?' He stood up and began making himself a cup of coffee while Georgie watched him with a slight frown. 'You led an old woman to believe a lie. In fact, worse than a lie because the idea is so utterly improbable.'

'For the best intentions!'

'Good intentions.' He snorted scornfully. 'The road to hell is paved with them. But that's as may be. The fact is she believes the fiction and palming her off with girlish tales isn't going to work.'

'Why not? Didi just needs a pick-me-up. I know it's all a charade, but it will get her out of the black hole and that's all that counts.'

'The means justifies the ends?'

'Something like that.'

'Well, we won't go into the sheer naïvety of that concept. The fact is, Didi expects more that just vague reports from you about secret assignations Heaven only knows where. Service stations on a motorway somewhere, I dare say. She insists that I come down for a long weekend…something about doing some Christmas shopping for you…'

Georgie blanched and he noticed her expression of dismay with a cynical acknowledgment of what was going through her head. Quite frankly, it was typical of her. She had embarked on something for the best possible, if totally misguided, reasons, and now her plan had taken on a life of its own and was beginning to drag her along in its unbridled wake.

'Come down?'

'That's right. And furthermore, she won't be fobbed off with vague, agreeable noises. In fact, this was the most insistent I have ever known her to be with me.'

'I can imagine.' Didi, whose own life had been vastly different from Pierre's, was in awe of her son's giddy and meteoric rise through the world of high finance, something about which she had virtually zero interest or understanding. She was also well aware of his deep seated disapproval of what he considered his parents' eccentric approach to money. Those two things combined had always meant that she tiptoed around him, solicitous but never quite relaxed enough for her to make demands.

'I won't bother to ask you what you mean by that. Suffice to say that my attempts to assure her that work is always at its most frantic in the time leading up to Christmas were ignored. In fact—' he had been vaguely surprised and amused at this '—I believe she told me at one point to shut up and do as I was told.'

'Oh, dear. That must have been a first for you.'

Pierre picked up the sarcasm in her voice, but when he looked at her her green eyes were wide and innocent and her expression oozed sympathy.

'The upshot is that a weekend is on the cards and you two, I gather, will be sharing secrets as you prepare a hot meal for the weary traveller when he arrives.'

'No.'

'Yes. Beginning to see the downsides to your brilliant scheme? Oh, sorry. Forgot you don't appreciate me referring to your idea as a *scheme*. Rubs in the deceptive element a little too strongly for your liking.'

'Well, it's a good sign that Didi's actually taking an interest in cooking,' Georgie said defensively. 'Do you remember what a fantastic cook she used to be?'

'Difficult for me to get a measure of that when I was at a boarding school,' Pierre said without any inflexion in his voice. 'At any rate, we're going to have to at least tally our stories.'

'I'm beginning to hate this,' she said miserably. 'It seemed just such an easy thing to say at the time. It was even kind of fun embellishing it! I never thought…*tallying stories*…I feel like a liar.'

'You *are* a liar. Worse, one who's prepared to drag other people into your lies…never mind there's already a woman in my life.'

'Sorry. And I'm sorry you cut short your evening because I landed on your doorstep.'

Pierre nodded curtly, although he was well aware that there had been no need to cut short anything. Jennifer, unwinding after a gruelling fortnight working on a deal that had been in the financial section of the newspapers off and on over the past month, had been prepared to enjoy the evening.

He, on the other hand, had found his mind drifting off to a certain slightly built, unruly, scatterbrained blonde waiting back at his house. He had barely been able to concentrate on a word Jennifer had been saying, even though some of the points she had been making about the intricate tax clauses she had had to revise had been quite interesting and pertinent to something he himself was currently working on. In fact, he had found his attention wandering to such an extent that he had finally succumbed and given up on the evening. To be resumed, he supposed, at a later date, when diaries had been consulted and schedules worked around.

'There was no need for you to feel guilty about leaving me here on my own,' she pressed, and Pierre let out a roar of laughter.

'Guilty? Me? For leaving you here on your own? Why should I feel guilty for leaving you here? For a start, you shouldn't have *been* here in the first place and, secondly, you could probably bludgeon an intruder to death with your line of small talk.'

'That's not very nice,' Georgie said, stung.

'No, it's not and I apologise. Unreservedly.'

'And I can tell you really mean that,' she told him coldly. 'So you want our stories to tally.'

'If we find ourselves in this fictional world of yours, then we might as well make it as plausible as possible. When exactly did our so called relationship start?'

'Some time ago. I may have mentioned six to eight months.'

'And tell me how it all happened. I'm keen to hear where your inventive mind took you.'

'To a fish restaurant in London the last time I was up.'

'You were up in London.'

'No, but I might have been and, if I *had* been, I might possibly have phoned you to see whether you wanted to go out for a drink.'

'Even though every time we have met in the past, we have ended up arguing over something or other?'

'Oh, for goodness' sake! Do you have to object to *everything* I say? Yes, we met for dinner! I had the…the cod and you had the tuna!'

'And after our suitably healthy meal…we repaired back to my place for some satisfying and frantic sex?'

Georgie went bright red. She actually thought that she could hear the blood slowly pumping through her veins and her skin went hot and tingly.

He sat there and his presence seemed to fill the kitchen, overwhelming her ability to think clearly.

Away from the familiar social situations in which they had met over the years, and stripped of the usual chaperons of mutual friends and family, she felt suddenly and agonisingly aware of herself as a woman, one he found at best amusing but not in a very funny way and, at worst, downright disagreeable.

And wasn't she living down to his every low expectation with her bizarre mode of clothing? Would any of his super-efficient girlfriends have undertaken a journey without packing a just-in-case change of clothing? Thereby finding herself at the mercy of a wardrobe several sizes too big for her? Guaranteed to make her look utterly ridiculous? No, no and no in answer to all three.

'I really haven't thought about the nuts and bolts in too much detail,' she said loftily. 'And I don't expect Didi will be asking prying questions about…about…anyway, we can just gloss over the exact times and dates we supposedly met up afterwards.'

'Why did I never come to see *you* in Devon?'

'Because you're incredibly selfish,' Georgie said waspishly, 'and that, I think, she *would* believe!'

Pierre leaned towards her and said softly, 'Stop right there, Georgie. *I* am doing *you* a favour, helping you out of the mess you've got yourself into. Yes, maybe it *will* do Didi some good, maybe it *will* give her something to look forward to, but I didn't have to do this. My life was going in a perfectly well-ordered direction without your meddling. So I advise you very strongly to keep that temper of yours in check!'

'Oh, very well,' Georgie mumbled, relieved when he drew back and gave her the chance to breathe a little easier.

'And as soon as Didi is back to her normal self, we tell her that things haven't worked out between us, got it? I'm not in this for the long haul.'

'Nor am I!' Her green eyes flashed, then she remembered

the 'keeping the temper in check' warning and subsided a little. 'Will you tell your girlfriend?' she asked curiously and Pierre shrugged.

'No need.'

'No need?'

'Ignorance is bliss. Have you never heard that saying?'

'Not when it pertains to something like this.'

'At any rate, she is not a vital part of my life. We see each other now and again. Enjoy each other. We both of us lead extremely busy lives, too busy to include a time consuming relationship.'

'Oh.'

For some reason her dumbfounded acceptance of this explanation was more annoying than if she had launched into one of her famous 'speak without thinking' monologues.

'You have a problem with that?' he asked irritably and Georgie, abiding by rules of detachment, hastened to assure him that she didn't, not at all.

'And I take it that there's no boyfriend lurking in the wings to clutter your little game plan?' His eyes sharpened on her because, to the best of his knowledge, she had never had a boyfriend, although, thinking about it, who was he to say? Recently he had seen very little of her on his trips to Devon, which, he reluctantly acknowledged, were few and far between.

'Not at the moment, no.'

'Has there ever been one?'

Georgie looked at him coldly, but something in her stirred with an odd mixture of hurt and resentment. She knew exactly what sort of women Pierre found attractive, just as she knew that, to him, she was little more than an overgrown tomboy. When he had been making his ambitious plans to leave Devon and make his mark in the city, she had been climbing trees and foraging the beach for driftwood, and later, when time had moved on and she no longer climbed trees, she had branched out in an even more incomprehensible way. Teaching had allowed her to avoid the boring uniform of the office bound woman. She wore trousers and flowing, comfortable clothes and did all the things he himself would never have deigned to do. She had always called it 'having fun' although, from what he had implied today, he too had fun in a completely different way.

'What do *you* think?' she asked, trying to inject a note of amusement in her voice although, to her own ears, she sounded sharp and offended.

'No idea.' He gave her a leisurely head-to-toe look that made her stomach do a little uncomfortable flip. 'I somehow never associated you with a raging sex life.'

'I don't conduct myself like that!'

'Like what?' Pierre found himself oddly interested in her vehement protest and, from nowhere, he recalled what he had thought for those first few seconds when he had seen her wearing his clothes. She was small and slender and the clothes drowned her, but she looked sexy for that. Something about that slightly dishevelled look, as if life was constantly taking her by surprise and delighting her.

'I don't do casual relationships for the sex, Pierre.'

'I thought all twenty-somethings did, or doesn't it work that way in Devon?'

'People in Devon are exactly the same as people anywhere else! There's no need to talk about us as if we evolved from another planet!' She felt herself building up to an explosion when she noticed that he was trying hard not to laugh. 'Very funny, Pierre,' she said sourly.

'You were saying…that you didn't believe in sex before marriage…'

'I never said any such thing and you know it!' She met those brilliant blue eyes and her stomach did another flip.

'I just don't have relationships the way you do. I don't go out with people because I need a bed partner ever so often. Anyway, whether I've had boyfriends or not is none of your business.'

'Oh, but it is…considering we're now an item! Surely I'm entitled to know about your past?'

Georgie was beginning to harbour regrets about her impulsive decision to involve him in a phony relationship. She had pigeon holed him as a good looking but boring man whose only concern was the business of making money. Okay, so maybe his only concern *was* the business of making money, but she was beginning to have glimpses of a far more complex individual than she had given him credit for.

'No, you're not,' she snapped. 'Although, and I don't know why I'm telling you this, but I *have* had several *exciting* relationships with some *very interesting* men.'

'Obviously not exciting enough to have held your attention in the long term.'

'So which weekend exactly do you have in mind to come to Devon?' Georgie, unsettled by his prodding, chose to change the subject completely. 'You mentioned a long weekend, but I guess your work commitments wouldn't allow that.'

'Do you mean you *hope* my work commitment wouldn't allow it?'

'I meant that if you can't find time to have a relationship with a woman, then how can you suddenly find time to have a mini-break in Devon?'

'Did I have a choice? You can't have really expected us to have a long-distance relationship until such time as Didi declared herself cured of her depression, did you?'

'I feel awful that you're deceiving your girlfriend.'

'Well, you should have contemplated that possibility

before you embarked on your bright idea, and, anyway, isn't it a tad hypocritical to talk to me about feeling guilty about Jennifer when you're happy to string Didi along?'

Georgie was silenced by that obvious truth, which didn't mean that she didn't give him a mutinous glare by way of response.

'Thinking about it, next weekend would suit me, to answer your original question. Like I said, I'll have to check my diary, but the sooner the better as far as I'm concerned.'

He looked at his watch. 'And now, I'm going to do a couple of emails and then I'm heading up to bed.'

'You're going to *work*?'

'Extraordinary, isn't it? For some of us, the working day never ends. And, by the way, I would offer you the loan of pyjamas, but I don't possess any...'

He disappeared out of the kitchen and Georgie made her way upstairs.

Having thoroughly and unashamedly explored the house in his absence, she knew where he would be working. She also knew where his bedroom was and now she found herself feverishly picturing him in his giant king-sized bed *without pyjamas*.

Had he made that passing remark about not possessing any just to make her feel uncomfortable, or was she reading too much into a throw-away statement of fact?

It struck her that she had been hopelessly naïve in her assumptions about Pierre.

She had nurtured a very handy one dimensional image of him, but the flesh and blood was turning out to be vastly different and strangely disturbing. Of course, his lifestyle was not one that she could really comprehend. Why spend all that time working to accumulate more money than could be reasonably spent in one person's lifetime? But he was hardly the automaton she had imagined.

And the possibility of his having a current girlfriend was one she had not even contemplated, although now, thinking about it, why ever not? The man was good looking and incredibly wealthy. He would have had no problem landing any woman he wanted. But still, she had travelled to London in the blithe belief that, deception or not, she was doing the right thing and therefore it would work out.

And now that he had been cornered into going along with her plan, she realised that it wouldn't be long before he really started disliking her for her interference in his life. Indeed, Lord only knew, he probably disliked her already, more than he previously had.

Sleep did not come easy.

She imagined him downstairs in his office, scowling at his computer or maybe calling his girlfriend because he surely couldn't be so cold hearted as to leave her totally out of the loop.

And then, what on earth were they going to tell Didi when it was all over? Georgie hadn't been lying when she had confessed to Pierre that that was something about which she had spared precious little thought. In her fear and anxiety over Didi's frame of mind, she had jumped feet first in at the deep end. Belatedly, she realised that she might find herself floundering in the water without a lifebelt anywhere near.

She woke the following morning to find the house empty, which was something of a relief.

There was a note on the kitchen counter from Pierre politely wishing her a safe trip to Devon and love to Didi. Georgie read it, then tossed it into the bin. Something about that aggressive, black handwriting made her shiver with apprehension.

And on the trip back down, with her book optimistically opened in front of her, she found herself frowning at the passing scenery outside and wondering just what she had let herself in for.

Then, even worse, she caught herself wondering what *he* was up to.

Mostly, though, she thought how her intrinsically soft nature had a habit of landing her in situations that had not turned out according to plan. She thought of the adopted goose five years previously, which had terrorised the postman so badly that she had been forced to fetch her own mail from the post office. In fact, there had been, over the years, a series of stray animals that had somehow ended up outstaying their welcome until, finally, she was left with only her chickens, thank heavens.

But this situation did not involve stray animals. It was dawning on her that this might turn out to be a situation that was a runaway car, and she might be wrong but didn't runaway cars always end up wreaking havoc?

CHAPTER FOUR

USUALLY when Pierre had visited his mother, and by his reckoning it had not been for at least five months, he had been driven. Freed from the tedium of the traffic, he had been at liberty to carry on working in the back seat of the Bentley, only surfacing when the car had pulled up the drive to the cottage.

Today he had chosen to drive himself. The words *Quick Escape* were there, somewhere, at the back of his mind.

He hadn't spoken to Georgie since their bizarre meeting a week ago. He hadn't trusted himself because, and it didn't matter how reluctant he was, he was now an accomplice to her hare brained scheme. She hadn't liked him using that particular word, but no other word fitted the bill better, particularly after the two conversations he had had with Didi, during which he had virtually been obliged to don a hard hat just to ward off the onslaught of misplaced excitement and hesitantly breathless curiosity.

The polite surface affection that had always existed between them had been breached and he had found himself on the back foot, not quite knowing how to deal with a mother who now seemed vibrantly interested in *him*. What had he been up to? How wonderful that he could have had the time to slowly nurture his relationship with Georgie, taking it a step at a time! How anxious she had always been that he worked too hard, that his priorities were in the wrong place! That he would never find the right woman to slow him down and make him realise that there was more to life than the inside of an office!

Since when had his mother ever given him lectures on his lifestyle? In fact, since when had she ever told him how she felt about the life he led? Of course, he had always suspected, but that was because he was clever enough to read behind the lines.

Any slim hope of retracting his story about fictional meetings and non-existent lovesick nights of stolen passion had evaporated faster than dew in hot sun.

And Pierre blamed Georgie. For once in a situation in which he exercised no control, he had spent the week fulminating, cursing himself for not sending the woman on her way the minute he had spotted her in the foyer of the gym, for forgetting just how flaky she was.

He had no idea how he was supposed to feign a relationship with a woman who irritated him beyond belief and he was pretty sure that he would have to do a good job at the pretence because Didi would be watching—watching and looking out for all those little signals that demonstrated two people being in love. As Pierre had never been in love, he would just have to run with his imagination, although the minute he thought about Georgie, and he had thought about her too much over the past week for his liking, his teeth snapped together in frustration.

He switched off his radio and efficiently connected his ear piece so that he could use his mobile phone hands free, then he punched in Georgie's home number, which she had kindly scribbled down for him and left by his telephone before leaving his house a week ago. It would have been a small technical hitch, he supposed, if he had been obliged to ask Didi for the telephone number of the woman he was supposedly head over heels in love with. One thing to smell a rat, another to see it hurtling at breakneck speed across the floor in front of your eyes.

She answered on the third ring, sounding a little out of breath, as if she had dashed to get the phone.

'Catch you in the middle of something, did I?' he drawled. He pictured her screeching to a halt in mid-run in front of the phone, her curly fair hair every which way, her mouth slightly parted, her green eyes startled at the invasion of the phone ringing. Teachers should be the most organised people on the face of the earth and, having been subjected to a series of eulogies from his mother on what a brilliant teacher she was, he assumed that there was an organisational gene somewhere inside her, but he had yet to spot it. She had always given him a very passable impression of someone who preferred life to surprise them, having obviously never worked out that life's surprises were generally best avoided.

'I was just on the way out.' Georgie had been half expecting his call, but even that wasn't enough to diminish the sudden racing of her heart as she heard his low, lazy voice down the end of the line. 'Where are you?'

'In my car driving down. Were you hoping that I had managed to think of a convenient excuse to get out of this weekend?'

'Your mother would never forgive you. She's looking forward to this more than she's looked forward to anything since your dad died.'

'I know. She told me.'

'I'm sorry.'

Pierre ignored that. He couldn't see the point of apologies, not now that the proverbial stable door was well and truly bolted and the runaway horse long since disappeared over the distant horizon.

'What can I expect when I get to Didi's house?'

Somehow it didn't *feel* the sort of conversation to have standing up and Georgie sat down, cross-legged on the ground in her small hallway. She had been on the verge of sticking on her thick, waterproof jacket, and now she laid it on her lap because the hall was cold.

'Oh, the usual.'

'Come off it, Georgie. I'm suddenly being treated like The Prodigal Son, so *the usual* isn't exactly appropriate, is it?'

Georgie cleared her throat nervously. 'A nice meal,' she said, thinking of the spread Didi had insisted on laying on, despite Georgie's protests that *she really shouldn't, no, really, please don't go to any bother, Pierre will hate it,* 'I think she just wants us to have a nice, relaxed time…'

'A tall order, given the circumstances.'

'It doesn't help if you carry on being angry with me.'

'I'm not angry, I'm resigned.'

'You mean, the way someone with a sore throat's resigned to the prospect of full-blown flu?'

'Except in this case the virus might just be around for longer than two weeks.' Although it was only a little after four, it was already dark, too dark to see the scenery slipping past. 'Where were you going?'

'I beg your pardon?'

'You said that you were on the way out.'

'I'm nipping back to the school for parents' evening. I should be finished by five-thirty and then I'm going straight over to Didi's to help her.'

'Help her with what?'

'Oh, just the meal.'

Pierre groaned under his breath.

'I know, I know,' Georgie said hurriedly. 'But you wouldn't believe how bright-eyed and bushy-tailed she is, Pierre! Look, I have to dash. I'll see you later!'

Pierre heard, in amazement, the sound of dial tone as she hung up on him, and he disconnected his cell phone with a sharp frown of displeasure.

He thought of her, riding that bike of hers to the village, even though the roads would be dark and treacherous because the temperatures were dropping fast. Maybe she would opt for the clapped-out old Mini instead, which, if memory served him correctly, had always protested with indignation every time it was called upon to do what it had been designed for. It was not a restful image. Nothing about the woman was restful and Pierre liked the company of restful women, women who didn't raise his blood pressure and make his head throb. He thought of Jennifer, calm, sophisticated, controlled, and immediately shoved the image out of his head because she was no longer on the scene anyway. He had finished with her two days ago over a snatched cup of coffee in a café halfway between his office and hers. Not ideal, but better than the telephone or, worse, text, which had almost been the route given that neither of them could spare the time. She had been shaken but her voice had been controlled as she had asked him crisply for the reasons for the break-up.

Naturally he hadn't told her the truth. It had seemed just too long-winded and complicated at the time and, anyway, she would have choked on her cappuccino.

He had been surprised that the break-up had not affected him the way he had anticipated. He had enjoyed her company, after all. Had even, at one point, idly contemplated her credentials for becoming a permanent feature in his life. He had expected to feel more than a vague, shameful sense of relief that perhaps she might have been a long-term disaster.

The journey was long, tedious and, in the developing dark and cold, required a lot of concentration, but still he didn't regret leaving his driver behind. Even the most conscientious of employees were prey to curiosity and the fewer people knew about the charade, the easier it would be to slip back into his disciplined, well oiled way of life.

It was a little after eight by the time he eventually made it to his mother's house, which sat a short distance from the village, up a picturesque path bordered with tall trees, which, in summer, were spectacular but in winter resembled long, graceful hands reaching up to the sky. Up ahead, he could see lights on and he steeled himself for the ordeal ahead.

She must have heard the sound of tyres on the gravel because the front door was flung open before the car had come to a stop and he saw his mother framed in the doorway, wearing dark, casual clothes, with a wrap round her shoulders.

She was smiling.

'Didi…' he said, coming towards her, his overnight bag in one hand, his computer case in the other. He leant down and kissed her on the forehead and was startled when she pulled him close to her for a hug. Then she stood back from him, her hands still on his shoulders, and looked at him as if seeing him for the first time.

'I'm so glad you're here, Pierre!'

'Don't act so surprised, Didi. I did tell you that I would be coming for the weekend.' Or rather, *she* had told *him* that he would be coming for the weekend.

'I thought you might have cancelled. You've been known to do that, but I guess there's more than just me here to attract you!'

Pierre grinned a little weakly. Georgie had been right on one score. His mother was glittering like a shiny bauble on a Christmas tree, utterly radiant.

'I suppose you're dying to see Georgie…she popped over a bit earlier to help but then went back to her place to change…said she felt a little grubby after parents' evening…probably wanted to slip into something a little less starchy for your benefit…' She drew him inside. 'I can't believe the pair of you kept this tucked up your sleeve for eight months!'

'Ah…' Pierre managed.

'Eight months! Now, I'm not going to pry or ask too many questions. I know you young people prefer to have your little secrets.'

'No truer word spoken,' Pierre murmured, thinking of the *little secret* he and his so-called beloved were sharing.

Inside the cottage were glorious smells. 'I hope you didn't put yourself out for me, Didi,' Pierre said. 'Georgie said that you…haven't been your usual self for a while. I wouldn't want you to overdo things…'

'I've got a new lease of life,' she confided. 'You go into the sitting room, darling, and I'll fetch you a glass of wine… unless you want to go and have a bath? You must be hot and bothered after that long drive. I'm surprised you didn't get Harry to bring you down. Surprised but glad. It'll be so special, just the three of us together…'

'Yes,' was all Pierre could manage this time, but it was enough to elicit another beaming smile from his mother as she ushered him into the sitting room and half pushed him onto the sofa so that she could bustle off and fetch him something to drink.

Left on his own, Pierre looked around the cosy room and noticed for the first time how many memories there were of his mother's past. Artifacts collected from travels over the years and little framed pictures everywhere. Usually he came, checked the house to make sure that everything was in order and would take his mother out for supper and the following day for lunch.

He strolled over to some of the pictures and realised that there were a lot of him, from childhood through to adolescence.

'I have boxes of them,' her voice from behind interrupted him and he turned around as Didi came to him with a glass of wine.

Pierre flushed. What touched him almost as much as the number of pictures was the fact that she obviously cleaned them, made sure that there was not so much as a speck of dust on the ornate silver frames.

He realised that he couldn't think of anything to say, but before he could be put in the position of finding a suitable response the doorbell buzzed and Didi almost giggled with delight.

No wonder Georgie had been overcome by impulse, drawn into putting a smile on Didi's face, whatever the cost. Still crazy, but he felt a twinge of comprehension.

There was the sound of voices and he strolled out of the sitting room to see Georgie, clutching a bottle of wine and a bunch of flowers and being divested of her coat and scarf.

Didi, puffed up with pride, stood to one side and Pierre thought, *to heck with it*. Georgie had dragged him unwittingly into this farce and he wickedly decided to teach her a little lesson.

He rested his glass on the table in the hall and went up to her, watching with wry amusement as the smile she had pinned on her face shifted from dutifully thrilled to see him to hesitantly bemused at his reaction.

'Here at last,' he breathed, taking her into his arms and curling his fingers into her fair hair. 'I thought you'd never arrive…'

Georgie was frantically trying to think of something suitably witty and light-hearted to say when she felt his lips touch hers and it was as if she had received a sudden electric shock. His mouth was firm and warm and this was no casual kiss. His tongue stole into her startled mouth, making her gasp, but when she would have shrunk back he held her firm, his hand gently controlling in the small of her back, forcing her to lean into him. By the time he pulled back, her thoughts had been scattered to all four winds and her heart was hammering like a drum inside her. She almost stumbled in her confusion and she could feel her face burning red when she met Didi's eyes.

'Young love. Your dad and I used to be like that. Couldn't keep our hands off each other when we were courting.'

'I know.' Pierre looked down at Georgie. 'We have the same problem, don't we, sweetheart?'

'Oh, yes!' Georgie said in a high-pitched voice while trying to edge away from him, but not getting very far because his arm had now snaked around her waist and was holding her firmly in place.

'How was your evening chatting to the parents?' he asked silkily, tightening his grip when he felt her trying to pull away. She felt girlishly fragile under her layers of clothing.

'Very good! Thank you! Didi, shall I pop these flowers in a vase for you?'

'Not at all. I'll do that. You two can disappear to the sitting room and catch up. I can still remember what it's like to be young, you know.' She smiled warmly. 'Besides, I have some last-minute cooking to see to if we're ever to eat tonight.'

As soon as Didi had disappeared towards the kitchen, Georgie sprang back and glared at him.

'What was that all about?' she hissed.

'It was all about us being in love,' Pierre answered innocently. 'Isn't that what we're supposed to be?'

'Yes, but…don't you think you were taking the performance a little *too far*?'

He shrugged and stepped back, allowing her to sweep past him into the sitting room where, he noticed, she made sure to take the only one seater in the room. He sat on the sofa and shook his head, patting the space next to him. When she tucked her legs under her, he sighed laboriously, stood up and went across to where she was looking at him nervously.

'Won't do.'

'What won't do?'

'You sitting all on your own over there. Not really the right image of a couple madly in love, is it?'

He had leant down to speak to her and, in the half light in the room, Georgie shivered, realising conclusively what she had managed to get herself into. This man didn't play by the rules.

'B-but we're not madly in love,' Georgie stammered. Her lips still tasted of him. She almost couldn't believe that he had done that, kissed her like that.

'Oh, but we are, when we're here.' They both heard Didi returning and he pulled Georgie quickly to her feet so that they were still entwined when his mother entered the room.

He feathered a kiss lightly on the crown of her head and Georgie was tempted to poke him soundly in the back because she knew just what he was doing. He didn't like her and he certainly didn't much care for the position in which he now found himself, but, beast that he was, he wasn't going to be the biddable force she wanted. He was going to make sure that she was hoist by her own petard. He ran a finger along her spine and she shivered and only managed to create a little distance between them when she accepted the glass of wine his mother was proffering to her, though not for long.

'Tell me all about these wonderful meetings of yours,' Didi encouraged as they sat on the sofa, Pierre's arm casually draped over her shoulders so that she was pulled against him. She had brought in a large platter of bites, which she assured them would have to do for starters. Prawns, little salmon rolls, bread sticks and a salsa dip in the middle. It gave Georgie a few seconds worth of time putting some of the delicacies on her plate to gather her thoughts together.

For someone of whom she intrinsically disapproved, the man was having a ridiculous effect on her nervous system.

Thank goodness she had dressed for the weather, lots of flowing layers, because she shuddered to think how her body might react if those arrogantly wandering hands of his came upon her bare flesh.

'Why don't you tell your mum all about it, *darling?*' She smiled sweetly at him over her shoulder and then edged away so that she could tuck into the food, which tasted delicious. Didi had done precious little cooking of late, and even though the salmon and prawns were not a complicated affair they tellingly revealed the change in her state of mind.

She looked encouragingly at Pierre. Safely out of range of physical contact, she felt her scattered nerves begin to haltingly regroup.

'Oh, the usual.' Pierre smiled at Didi's eager expression and helped himself to a mountain of titbits. 'Looks good, Didi. Have a lie-in in the morning. I'll bring you a cup of tea and some toast.' It would be a first for him, cooking breakfast for someone else, and it was hardly an invitation to fly to the moon, but he was awkwardly aware that he had delivered a mighty treat, judging from his mother's radiant smile. It had never occurred to him that such a small gesture could evoke such a richly rewarding response. Normally he woke with the larks when he was in Devon so that he could download his emails and catch up on whatever he might have missed the night before while his mother snoozed. Often he would grab a slice of toast long before she had awakened and would keep her company in the kitchen while she ate, his mind half on whatever deal he happened to have on at the moment.

'Goodness, Pierre! There's no need to, although it *would* be lovely…'

'You were about to tell your mum how we met…I haven't exactly been forthcoming with details, have I, Didi?' Georgie turned fully to Pierre and shot him a look implicit with meaning. 'I thought you'd like to hear it from Pierre himself. I know he's not terribly—hmm, now what's the word?—*open* when it comes to expressing himself…but I just *know* how much he's been dying to fill you in…'

Georgie wondered what he would say. They had not communicated during the week and she knew that he would have been simmering at the uncomfortable position in which he had unwittingly found himself. She could apologise until the cows came home and it would make no difference. He would still be angry with her. Even though he must surely see the beneficial effects of their little deception. Didi had blossomed. Once her strength and purpose had returned, then, yes, they could decide how to break it to her that their relationship was over. She would be able to cope.

Georgie had only vaguely contemplated this scenario. She preferred to live in the present and appreciate its rewards rather than dwell on situations still yet to occur.

'She chased me,' Pierre said, looking at her from under his lashes as he sipped the wine. 'Like a shameless hussy—'

'Hang on!'

'Georgie!' Didi exclaimed, tickled pink by her son's outrageous lie.

'I think *chase* is a bit strong, *darling*.'

'Nonsense.' He deposited his empty plate on the table and relaxed back into the sofa, linking his fingers behind his head so that he could watch her through half-closed eyes. Georgie couldn't imagine how she could ever have found this man *boring*. Since when was *dangerous* boring? She wondered at the countless times in the past when she had taken him to task over his parents. She had never felt the hairs on the back of her neck stand on end then as they did now. But then she had never in the past *invaded his life*, had she? Yes, she had irritated the hell out of him, but this was a different situation, wasn't it?

'Oh, there's nothing wrong with the woman making the first move!' Didi said delightedly, leaning forward in her chair, her hands pressed together. Where Pierre was tall and forbidding, his mother was delicate and warm, only their strikingly swarthy complexions linking them as mother and son. Her eyes were shining.

'I think Pierre might be exaggerating just a tad!' Georgie said, cornered.

'You called me, don't you remember?' Pierre raised his eyebrows in unbidden amusement. 'You said that you were in town and were at loose ends for dinner…sounds like an invitation to me…' He gave his mother a conspiratorial look, which tickled her pink. 'Naturally, what could a gentleman do?' he asked with a casual shrug of his broad shoulders.

Georgie cast her mind back to the gentleman who had greeted her at his gym with barely concealed hostility and impatience, as if a yapping dog had suddenly materialised clinging to his tailor-made Italian trousers.

The gentleman, it turned out, was more than prepared to be open about the winding course of their relationship. Georgie would never have credited him with the imagination, which showed how perilous it was to imagine you knew someone when you had only skimmed the surface, she decided.

Over dinner, which was tasty and hot and filling and washed down with liberal amounts of white wine, which Didi must have had delivered earlier in the day, he expanded on dates they had never had, kisses they had never shared, a love of theatre, which she supposed they might well have shared if given half a chance. She barely managed a word in edgewise.

Eventually, he gave her a secretly satisfied half-smile. Georgie, in return, grinned wanly at Didi.

'It's late, isn't it?' She yawned widely. 'Why don't you and Pierre catch up, Didi, and I'll tidy the kitchen?'

Eight o'clock had turned into midnight. Didi, as if suddenly waking up to reality, walked to the kitchen window, pulled up the blinds, which had kept the winter night at bay, and turned to Georgie with a frown.

'Georgie, darling, how did you get here?'

'Drove,' Georgie said, surprised. She got up and walked across to the window and stared out in dismay. The cold snap had finally broken and the snow that had been threatening for the past four days was falling down over the fields, the trees, everything. Including her car. 'I'm going to have to go, Didi,' she said, in a panic.

'You can't drive back, Georgie,' Didi said firmly. 'Can she, Pierre?' She glanced over to her son for back-up and he dutifully joined them at the window, where he fell silent at the sight of the snow. It hardly ever snowed in London. He had forgotten what a beautiful sight it was.

'Absolutely not,' Pierre said, meaning it. He looked at Georgie. 'Your car's never been noted for its reliability. In this weather, I should think all it wants is tucking up in a warm garage and a cup of hot chocolate.'

Georgie couldn't help herself. She laughed, because the description was so damned accurate.

'I keep telling her that she should get rid of it, but you're fond of that old thing, aren't you, dear?' Didi made a half-hearted effort to bustle towards the kitchen sink but, as though suddenly aware of the passage of time, it was obvious that her energy was flagging and she looked relieved when Georgie insisted she go upstairs and get some sleep.

'And you won't be attempting that trip back, will you?' Didi asked anxiously from the door and Georgie shook her head with a reassuring smile.

'I wouldn't dream of it. I'll make up the guest room, Didi. I know where everything is.'

'Don't be silly.' Didi waved the suggestion down. 'I'm not your Victorian maiden aunt, Georgie, and there's no need to go bright red. I know what happens between two young adults in love!'

Georgie, trying hard not to look appalled at what was inevitably coming, pinned a wooden smile on her face.

'You and Pierre,' Didi announced, backing out of the kitchen with a yawn, 'can share. You'll just need to fetch a fresh towel from the airing cupboard and I'll see you both in the morning!'

Georgie turned slowly to Pierre as soon as the kitchen door was shut and glared at him.

'This is *your* fault!' she hissed accusingly.

'I've been blamed for many things in my time,' he said coolly, 'but never for the weather.'

'I'm not talking about the snow and you know it.' She began clearing the table. It had been a one-pot meal, so at least not too many dishes. Didi didn't possess a dishwasher, which she associated with somehow deeply endangering the environment and aiding and abetting global warming, so Georgie began filling the sink with hot water, not even looking in Pierre's direction because the minute she did she knew that she would also, in her mind's eye, have a sickening vision of him alongside that big king sized bed that was in his bedroom.

Pierre swung her around to face him and his face was like granite.

'Don't even think of doing the maidenly outrage act, Georgie!' His voice was soft and silky and as cutting as a whip.

'I know I got us into this, Pierre. You haven't failed to remind me of that every step of the way but...'

'But? You're suddenly finding the consequences of your actions a little too uncomfortable for your liking?'

Georgie looked at him mutinously and found herself being

distracted by his eyes. Amazing eyes and fabulously long, thick, dark eyelashes. The sort of eyelashes any woman would have given her right arm for. No wonder those brainy women he favoured had also all been stunning. He could have it all. The brains and the beauty. She blinked and forced herself back to the reality of him gripping her shoulders and glaring at her while the yellow rubber gloves she was wearing dripped water on the flagstone floor around her.

'But you didn't have to go overboard with the lovey-dovey act.'

'But isn't that what we're *supposed* to be?' he asked in a voice that dripped sarcasm. 'Madly in love? I was only playing to my brief, after all.'

And it's all your doing was the rider to that observation, unspoken but as clear as a bell.

'And don't even think about getting into that sewing machine of a car of yours and trying to drive back to your cottage in this weather.'

'I wasn't,' she said sulkily. 'But if you were any kind of gentleman, you would offer to drive me. *Your* car could handle the trip easily.'

'But I'm no gentleman,' Pierre said without batting an eyelid. He abruptly released her and stood back, shoving his hands in his pockets and observing her with apparent fascinated interest. 'We're in this ridiculous situation together…' his mouth quirked with the irony of what he said next '…for better and for worse, so you might as well resign yourself to the fact. And I'm really surprised that you're not a little more pliable,' he murmured, 'considering you went to such lengths to nab me in the first place.' He grinned as angry colour streamed into her cheeks. 'I mean, phoning my office when you were in London, inveigling your way up to the directors' floor and waiting two hours for me to finish my meeting so that you could invite me to dinner...' He had never thought himself to be creative, but he had certainly risen to the task of describing their fictitious love affair with astounding inventiveness and he had thoroughly enjoyed every minute of the storytelling. 'Then those jazz tickets you managed to get hold of, knowing that I would be tempted to go with you...worked, though, didn't it? You landed your man!'

'How *could* you invent all those stories?'

'That's rich, coming from the Queen of Invention!'

Georgie, without much of a leg to stand on, didn't say anything.

'Tut-tut, no need to look so hot and bothered,' Pierre soothed. 'As Didi said, this *is* the twenty-first century and there's nothing wrong with the woman doing all the running. Now—' he looked at his watch and then back to her '—I'm going to do an hour's work so that's a headstart for you, and if you're in need of some sleepwear you can always borrow one of the tee shirts I keep here in the cupboard. Be a nice touch, don't you think? Wanting to wrap yourself up in your man's clothes so that you can breathe him in?'

'Hilarious. I never knew you had such a sense of humour.' It would be a mad rush finishing the kitchen and scrambling to be safely asleep before he waltzed into the bedroom, but it could be done. With any luck, she would be fast off by the time he headed up and oblivious to his presence.

She sprang into immediate action the minute he was out of the kitchen, flying through the remainder of the dishes at speed and with a good forty minutes to spare before he finished doing whatever he was doing downstairs. She had no idea how anyone could contemplate sitting in front of a computer at such a ridiculous hour but she wasn't about to complain.

As she drew the thick, light obliterating velvet curtains, the snow was still falling steadily outside, a thick layer of eerie, pristine white over the fields that stretched behind the house.

The bedroom, in which she herself had slept a couple of times in the past when Didi had had friends to stay and had wanted her help, was not large. The bed dominated the room. There was a small old-fashioned mahogany wardrobe with a mirrored front, a chest of drawers on which a bowl of pot pourri released a fragrant scent, and a little dressing table by the window, which overlooked the open fields. No handy sofa bed. No sofa, in fact.

And more galling was the fact that she actually did end up in one of his tee shirts and it did, in some obscure way, smell of him, a peculiar tangy, fresh and utterly masculine scent that filled her nostrils.

She closed her eyes and in the darkness felt her skin tingle at that fleeting, remembered touch of his mouth on hers.

It wouldn't do!

Making sure that she was on the furthest side of the large bed, she resolutely thought about school and the nativity play that they were rehearsing and in the end, when that failed to work, she fell back on the age old *sheep* until her brain stopped whirring and sleep kicked in.

CHAPTER FIVE

PIERRE wasn't sure whether he would find Georgie awake and huddled at the side of the bed experiencing an attack of the vapours, or else pretending to be asleep, but actually when he finally hit the bedroom it was to the even breathing of someone fast asleep.

The curtains blocked out what little outside light there was and it took him a few seconds just staring in before his eyes acclimatised to the darkness.

Then something constricted inside him because, not only was she soundly asleep, she had also worked her way out of the duvet and he could make out one slender thigh resting provocatively on top.

Very quietly he closed the bedroom door, not wanting to wake his mother, aside from anything else. He had already showered using the bathroom on the landing because the cottage was glaringly devoid of anything as up-to-date as a guest room with *en suite*. As a courtesy to his bed companion, he had worn boxer shorts to bed, in the absence of any pyjamas, and a tee shirt.

Which, judging from what he could see, replicated her own nightwear save for the boxer shorts.

He grinned in the darkness. So she *had* resorted to using

one of his tee shirts. He grinned even more as he recalled her outraged expression when he had provoked her by insinuating that she might want to have the smell of him on her. She was remarkably easy to wind up and had the sort of expressive face that showed every passing emotion. Not cool, not calm, not collected, but not the sort whose company could ever put a man to sleep.

Pierre slipped under the covers and then arranged them carefully back over her sprawled body and stiffened when she tossed beside him. She had obviously started off at the very edge of the bed, probably with her body half spilling over the mattress, he suspected, but in the course of her sleep had worked her way to somewhere near the middle, and he wasn't about to shift her back into her original position of self-defence.

There was no reason why their bodies couldn't come into contact without them exploding with a sudden onslaught of lust.

Indeed, the thought was almost laughable!

Pierre was no ingénue when it came to the opposite sex. Boarding school might have been dreary but it had given him a great deal of polish from an early age, and the addition of girls in the sixth form had honed his ability to charm to a fine degree. The self-confidence of maturity and his astounding good looks had meant that women had always flocked towards him. He had never had to work at getting a woman into bed. He had certainly never joined a woman in bed to find her sound asleep!

But this, he told himself, was no *woman*, at least not in the sense in which it was meant.

He propped himself on one elbow and looked down at her. His eyes were now quite accustomed to the lack of light and he could make out her delicate features, her mouth slightly parted, her slim arm carelessly resting on the duvet, her hand balled into a light fist.

His eyes strayed down and he lay back flat, staring upwards at the ceiling.

He hadn't asked for this but things had certainly changed since undertaking the pretence. His mother had never been so open with him before. Holidays spent as a youngster had been largely lonely affairs until he was old enough to start inviting friends to stay and he wondered whether he had gradually built up a wall of resentment when in fact it hadn't been a question of love, simply a question of his parents working all hours on the farm. Had they tried to include him? He couldn't remember. He could only remember growing up with a strong sense of disapproval of the fruitless road along which they had chosen to travel.

He wasn't much given to introspection, but it occurred to him that many a worthwhile relationship floundered through lack of communication and, really, by the time he *could* effectively communicate with his parents on an adult level, they had probably only seen a man with little to say that was encouraging or optimistic.

He could distinctly remember lecturing to them about the futility of sinking money into a niche farming market that would end up draining them of funds and advising them to go into property instead, which had naturally led to the tired old argument about capitalism. He had given up and thenceforth had learnt to skim the surface when it came to conversation, always slightly relieved when he returned to the gruelling demands of his life in the City.

And so the pattern had continued down the years. Until now.

He turned away from Georgie. Sleep came easily. He was tired. A long day driving, then an hour and a half spent on the computer before heading up to the bedroom. He would still be up at the crack of dawn because that just seemed to be how his body clock worked, but that was several hours away.

He woke when it was still dark to the very slightest of noises. More a sensation of movement than a noise, in actual fact, and was instantly awake.

Silhouetted in the doorway, and just a dark, slight figure, Georgie was creeping towards the bed, groping to feel the edge of the landmarks in the room that would stop her from tripping.

'You can turn the lights on if you want,' Pierre said dryly and Georgie let out a little squeak of shock.

'What are you doing awake?'

Pierre switched on the lamp on his bedside table and followed her progress as she scuttled back under the duvet, all pink-faced, rumpled femininity.

'You can turn the light off now. I just had to use the bathroom. I'm going back to sleep.' Georgie turned pointedly onto her side and yanked the duvet as high up as it could go without her toes protruding at the bottom.

'I'm a very light sleeper,' Pierre answered her question even though it was clear that she wanted to feign sleep. He, on the other hand, felt fully awake and he knew why. It was nearly six, close to his natural waking-up time. 'I think it's because every holiday I would return from boarding school to the farm and could never quite manage to adjust to the sound of the animals. When you're not used to sheep and owls it's surprising how noisy they can seem.' He noticed, with amusement, that she was still lying with her back to him and her body was rigid.

He had not been looking forward to this long weekend. It was time he couldn't spare from the demands of work and for a reason that was not of his doing. When he visited his mother, his trips were planned long in advance, giving him the appropriate time to rearrange his schedule.

However, he reluctantly had to admit that it was not the ordeal he had anticipated.

He certainly hadn't anticipated ending the evening in bed

with Georgie and, furthermore, if he was to be honest with himself, vaguely intrigued by her.

He had a sudden, sharp urge to surprise her out of her pointed silence, some mischievous desire that wasn't *at all* like him.

'I decided to break up with Jennifer…' He dangled this personal snippet of information in front of her eyes and waited for her to respond. Which she did. She also rolled over so that she was now facing him and, even though he was staring upwards, his head resting on his linked hands, he was very much aware of her eyes on him.

'I'm sorry about that.'

'Why? I told you it was nothing serious. No…I just thought that it would have been a little unfair to keep her dangling on a string while I passed the time with another woman.'

'Hardly *passing the time with another woman*…'

'No?' He turned his head so that he was looking at her. It was still very dark in the room, no sign yet of a rising sun, but he was aware that she was very close to him. In fact, he could almost smell her and she smelt sweet, innocently sweet of fruity soap and recently washed hair. Not a hint of perfume, which he rather liked. 'We're sharing a bed, aren't we? What would you call that?'

'I would call it your mother combined with an unexpected snowstorm!'

'Do you know that you're the first woman I've ever slept with?' Pierre hadn't meant to confess to that. He surprised himself.

'Oh, *please*. You must think I was born yesterday if you imagine that I could actually believe that—'

'What's so unbelievable about it?'

'Pierre Christophe Newman *has never slept with a woman*…? Ha, ha. That's like saying that Casanova actually did embroidery in his spare time!'

'Is that what you think I am? A Casanova?'

Georgie's breath caught in her throat. Even in the darkness of the bedroom, there was no mistaking his sheer beauty, that animal magnetism that he unconsciously radiated in waves. There was also no mistaking the fact that her nerves were everywhere as the intimacy of their situation impacted. She could feel her body tingling all over, from her face to her breasts to the very essence of her.

'I think it's time we tried to grab a bit more sleep or…or maybe I could see what the snow's doing…drive back home…it's probably cleared by now…'

'Don't be farcical,' Pierre said with squashing practicality. 'What's Didi going to think when she emerges from bed to find that you've disappeared into the snow at the crack of dawn? Besides, we're supposed to be a hot item—the least we could do is make conversation.'

'In bed?'

'I happen to find bed a very relaxing place and, to clarify what I meant about having never slept with a woman, I meant spent the night in the same bed.'

'You've *never spent the night with a woman*?' Georgie asked incredulously. Okay, she knew that curiosity killed the cat but she just couldn't help herself.

The ploy successfully distracted her and he could sense her relax as she stopped thinking about the intimacy of their situation, which she minded but he rather thought he didn't. 'No need to sound so stupefied,' Pierre told her but, seeing it from her point of view, it *was* a little mysterious.

'How come?'

'Have *you* ever spent the night with a man?'

'We're not talking about me and I'm not a…a…'

'Casanova?' He felt her discomfort. This was invigorating. 'I don't like waking up next to a woman.'

'You mean just in case it gives them crazy ideas of permanence?' Georgie asked shrewdly.

Pierre stiffened. 'Do I hear a lecture on its way?'

'It's too early for lectures but, yes, if it had been a little later, there *would* have been a lecture.'

Pierre wondered what book she had studied on the Art of Seducing Men, where surely rule one would have been *Think before you speak*, but then she wasn't in the business of seducing him, was she? In fact, she was in the business of avoiding him as much as was humanly possible given the circumstances. 'I keep irregular hours when it comes to my work,' he perversely felt the need to elaborate. 'Makes sense not to have someone else to think about when I'm climbing out of bed at three in the morning to make a long-distance conference call to the other side of the world.' No response. 'Women tend to dislike awakening to the peal of the telephone and the lights being switched on at ridiculous hours in the morning.' Still no response and her silence had a judgemental tone that was really beginning to get on his nerves. 'And maybe you're right,' he ground out bad-temperedly. 'Maybe I *don't* want some woman thinking that a night in my bed is the start of something long-term.'

Georgie grunted with what he considered a lot of smug satisfaction.

'Anyway, now that we're on the road of discovery, have *you* ever spent the night with a man?'

'Of course I have.'

Pierre was unnaturally shocked by that admission. She was the tomboy who had grown up into a ditzy woman who taught young kids and kept chickens! Where did sleeping around figure in this scenario? Furthermore, night life was sorely lacking in this particular part of the world. Where on earth would she have rummaged up an eligible male?

Not that she wasn't pretty in her own way, he considered.

Some men might even find that blonde, fly-away hair and those huge green eyes quite attractive. Less so her habit of acting first and thinking later, but, then again, who knew? Impulsive might appeal to some kind of men. The backpacking, camping-site sort probably. The ones who woke up on a sunny Friday, decided that the skies were blue and thought nothing of calling in sick so that they could head out for a bracing walk on some remote Devon path somewhere.

'Surprised?' Georgie asked.

'Of course not!' Pierre lied smoothly. 'Why should I be? Most women of your age have probably had more than one man spend the night in their bed. Who was he? Anyone I know?' His voice was light, mildly interested but no more than mildly. He would never have admitted that his curiosity had been piqued.

'I didn't think you kept in touch with anyone from this part of the world, Pierre. I thought you had jettisoned the lot the minute you left for the bright city lights.'

'Why do you always imply that ambition is somehow a bad thing?' He lay flat, head resting on his folded arms, and stared up at the ceiling while Georgie propped herself on one elbow and stared at him. On a subconscious level there was something dangerous and exhilarating about this whispered conversation, but she refused to be alarmed because *really* that was all it was. A conversation. *Useful* conversation, in fact, considering the game they were playing.

'Is that what I do?'

'You know it is, Georgie. And I wonder why that would be. Is it because you've always been so scared of leaving this place that your only defence is to criticise the people who do? I mean, your parents died when you were too young to really be able to look after yourself and mine have always been the substitute. Is that why you've always felt the need to stay here? Because this is the place where all your security is wrapped up?'

'I thought you didn't care for psychobabble, Pierre,' she said coldly. She lay back, like him, and stared sightlessly at the ceiling. 'I don't *criticise* people who choose to leave here. I'm not a fool! I know people want to do the best for themselves and sometimes that means leaving for a city!'

'But in my case...'

'I want to go to sleep now.'

Pierre pictured her lying next to him and squeezing shut her eyes so that she could block out the conversation. 'You won't be able to.'

'What do you mean?'

'I mean we're both fully awake now.'

'Which means that you should be thinking of doing a spot of work, doesn't it?'

Normally, yes, Pierre thought, but for once he felt inclined to break with tradition. 'Not sure I can brave the deep cold to get to my computer. There are only so many things I'm prepared to do in the name of work and frostbite isn't one of them.'

Georgie felt a small, reluctant smile threaten her defences. Damn man!

And while she was battling with a desire to relent, he swept in. 'So...? Was this man someone you were involved with for a long time? Was it a serious relationship?'

Georgie didn't see any point in being coy or secretive. Didi would find it very odd if Pierre knew nothing of her past when they were so in love that presumably every nook and cranny of their pasts had been explored in loving depth. Hilarious when you considered that this man was a commitment-phobe who made sure he never shared his bed with any woman just in case she took it as a sign that their next trip out would include buying matching wedding rings!

'Quite serious,' she admitted awkwardly.

Pierre was intrigued. He turned to look at her profile. For someone who seemed as transparent as a glass of water, she was certainly turning out to be far more complex than he had ever imagined.

'Really?' he coaxed.

'We even considered marriage at one point,' Georgie confessed.

'What happened?'

'Life happened.' She shrugged. It had taken time for the hurt to go away but eventually it had gone and she could look back now at Stan as something charming that had been just right at the time but would never have lasted in the long run. 'We met at university and fell in love and had two great years, but it didn't work out.'

'And that's all there is?' Pierre prodded.

'I don't give *you* the third degree over your girlfriends,' Georgie told him irritably. 'Yes, that's all there is to it!'

'Where is he now?'

'Married with a child and living on the other side of the world, I gather.'

'Ah.'

Georgie waited for him to expand on that knowing exhalation but he didn't.

'What does *that* mean?' she demanded finally. She turned on her side to find him right in front of her.

'Means that you must have been emotionally devastated,' he said, shamelessly prying for more details. 'Young, vulnerable, trusting and in love and, not only does it all collapse, but the man of your dreams heads off to the distant blue yonder and finds himself another woman and, to cap it all, has a baby with her. Is that why you're on your own? Too hurt to trust another man?'

'I think it's time we got up.'

'Not even the birds are up yet.' She looked incredibly young. How was it that he had never noticed that before? True she was younger than most of his ex girlfriends, but even so she looked light years less hard and experienced. Lawyers and barristers and investment bankers, he concluded, showed the stress of their jobs in their faces even when those faces appeared flawless. 'Are you still hankering after him?' If he took off without a backward glance, Pierre could just imagine the sort of man he had been. Irresponsible, one of those so-called free spirits who drifted where the wind happened to take them, probably had ambled off to find his spiritual nirvana somewhere in Tibet only to bump into a similarly woolly headed creature along the way. The man had probably had a beard and wore sandals in winter. The image of Georgie with someone like that was suitably satisfying.

'What did he do? What was his job? Did he have one?'

'Of course he had a job, Pierre! He was in his final year at university and went on to become a journalist. In fact, he left to cover a piece on global warming and the effects in Australia and just…found someone else out there… We still keep in touch now and again by email…'

'If you were that much in love with the man, why didn't you go with him?' Pierre, admittedly a little rattled by the fact that she had fallen for a guy with both feet planted firmly on the ground, was in like a shot.

'Because…' Because the thought had been too scary, because the relationship was already beginning to raise more questions than it answered, because her safety was in Devon and she had been loath to cut the apron strings, just as Pierre had said even if he had been taking pot-shots in the dark, trying to piece her together because there was nothing better to do just at this moment. 'Because I still had my university career to get through,' Georgie told him flatly. She could have added that she had taken away one very important lesson from the experience. People left and, when it came to men, she would make sure she fell in love with a man she could depend on, a man who didn't leave. She made as if to get out of the bed but Pierre beat her to it, even though it was damned cold because the central heating hadn't as yet been timed to kick in. His mother couldn't possibly be counting pennies–he provided her with enough money to keep the heating on full whack every day of the year if the desire so took her—but she was economical from habit. He just hadn't realised the effects until he pulled on his jumper, rubbing his hands together to keep warm.

'No need to run away, Georgie,' he drawled, slinging on his trousers, watching her watching him and sensing her embarrassment even though he had been wearing more than he would have worn on a beach.

'I wasn't about to run away,' Georgie lied, riveted by the sight of him getting dressed.

'I'll switch the heating on. This place is like a freezer. What's Didi playing at?'

Georgie heard herself mumble something but she was too busy watching him as he lounged indolently by the door to think coherently. There was something very real and yet very *unreal* about the situation. The sooner he headed downstairs to work, she thought, flustered, the better off she would be.

She flopped back onto her pillow the minute he had left the room.

It was later than she had first imagined. Nearly seven o'clock and already, in the space of only a short while, beginning to grow lighter. Without it looking fishy, she could conceivably start getting dressed and be out of the house by eight to feed the chickens and start working on some of the costumes, then maybe pop over later in the morning, perhaps stay for lunch. Didi knew that she was very busy with school activities. Christmas was just around the corner and there was always a flurry of things that needed doing before the school holidays began. She had made sure to warn her that there would be bits of the weekend when she would have to disappear. Tactfully, she had omitted to mention just what these *bits* were and how often they would occur.

But for the moment…

She hurried down to the bathroom, as quietly as she could, so that she could wash her face and swish her mouth with toothpaste, in the absence of a toothbrush. She wondered whether she should start carrying a little holdall every time she stepped foot out of her house, working on the assumption that she would inevitably end up stranded wherever she went and would therefore need a change of clothes, a toothbrush and some make-up.

It would be back into the clothes she had worn the evening before, face scrubbed clean, her blonde hair loosely gathered into a pony-tail.

The room was already beginning to warm up, which meant that Pierre must have advanced the heating. The entire house had been re-plumbed at the time of purchase and the central heating worked like a dream, unlike hers, which clattered noisily into life with the same reluctance to do its job as her car.

With her back to the door and safe in the knowledge that Pierre was sitting in front of a computer somewhere in the cottage, probably now totally oblivious to his surroundings, Georgie stripped off her borrowed nightwear and began sorting out her clothes, first checking to see whether the snow was still falling. It was, but less aggressively than the night before. She should be able to make it back to her place provided her car co-operated.

She turned away from the window, her mind chewing over the problem of how she could beat an exit without it appearing indecently hasty for someone who should be joined to her new-found love at the hip.

And there he was. She hadn't heard the door being pushed open, hadn't even been aware that she had left it very slightly ajar, not wanting the click to rouse Didi who needed her beauty sleep more than she cared to admit.

Shock raced through her, taking away her instinct to shield her naked breasts. She just stood there, her mouth parted, her hands limply at her sides. He was carrying a tray on which were two mugs of coffee and some toast.

He walked in and the freeze-frame shattered. Georgie covered her breasts, cheeks bright red with anger and sheer mortification.

'What are you doing up here?' she yelped. 'You're supposed to be downstairs! Working! *You said so!*'

'I said nothing of the sort.' Pierre rested the tray on the bed, then straightened up. 'I'll look away if you want to put something on, although it's a bit like shutting the stable door after the horse has bolted. Anyway, it's not as if I haven't seen a naked woman before...' But not this one. Oh, no. He had done his damnedest to make his voice as neutral as possible, but he felt as if he could see right through those protective hands trying to shield her nudity, see right through to the vision that had confronted him when he had walked into the bedroom.

She was as slim as he had expected and her breasts small and pert, tipped invitingly with rosy nipples that had made his powerful body surge into immediate response.

Nothing like any of the women he had dated in the past, who had, without exception, been taller and more curvaceously built.

She had the sort of body that exquisitely matched her personality—young, girlish, somehow innocent.

He turned away, frowning at his own dramatic response to

her, waiting while she stuck on her shirt and skirt, the whisper of clothes telling its own story of someone trying to get dressed as quickly as was humanly possible.

Eventually he turned round to find her in the same position but this time fully clothed, arms rigidly folded. She had pulled back the curtains and thin winter sunlight gave the room a cool, spectral greyness.

'I told my mother that I would bring her breakfast in bed. I didn't go downstairs to work. I went to make some coffee and toast.'

'You should have said!'

'You mean *asked your permission*?' He strolled towards her. 'You're trembling like a leaf,' he murmured, putting his hands on her arms and feeling her stiffen under him. A feeling of being utterly out of his depth and liking it rushed through his body, leaving him shaken and disconcerted. Her skin was as soft as a peach.

'Get off,' Georgie mumbled wildly, but her body wilfully refused to take evasive action. Instead, she remained standing still with her fingers biting into the soft flesh of her arms while his hands on her continued to sear her skin.

Pierre ignored her protest. It was meaningless anyway. Her voice might be telling him to leave her but her body was singing a different song.

And he, to his bemusement, felt as randy as a teenager. 'Why?' he asked softly, 'Is that what you really want me to do?'

'Yes!' Georgie said weakly. 'Of course it is,' she added, frantic to convince herself as much as him.

Pierre undid the pony-tail and pushed his fingers into her hair and Georgie drew in her breath, partly shocked by the gesture but mostly floundering in confusion, hopelessly trying to figure out what to do and to actually do it.

'You have beautiful breasts.' He bent and nuzzled her

face with his mouth, which elicited a moan from her. 'Can I touch them?'

Georgie, beyond speech, didn't say anything. She wanted this man so badly she was literally shaking from it. When did this happen? When did she hand over control of her mind to someone else? She felt his hand drop to her waist, slip underneath the loose-fitting top, the first of the many layers she wore in winter, rather than simply two with a coat.

'I'll take that as *yes,* then…' He slipped his hand higher until it brushed the rounded underside of her breast. 'No bra…was that because you were in such a rush to fling something on?'

'This is crazy,' Georgie struggled out.

'What is? You forget how madly in love we are…'

'We're not madly in love…you know that…we just…we mustn't…'

'We just…we mustn't…' Pierre mimicked her with a low, sexy laugh, 'but what if we want to?' He had resisted for too long. He cupped her soft breast with his hand, kneading it gently and rotating his finger over her stiffened nipple. She was as turned on as he was! He could feel her melting against him, incapable of stopping what he was doing to her body.

It was just as well because he wasn't sure whether he *could* stop if he wanted to, not now, not when he was hard and throbbing for her.

He unbuttoned the long-sleeved pale blue patterned shirt and spread it apart so that he could drink in the sight of her, as naked as when he had interrupted her in the middle of dressing, but this time she wasn't wearing that panicked look of a rabbit caught in the headlights. Nor was she rushing to cover herself. But she *was* breathing quickly, and looking down, not meeting his eyes. He tilted her face so that she had to look at him.

'Are you as turned on as I am?' he demanded roughly. She

looked as though, if only she could fight it, she would have walked away but she couldn't. She was as helpless as he was to the charged electricity between them.

To think that she had slept with another man, had a two-year relationship with him! Walked into his outstretched arms of her own volition and not because her body was obeying its own urgent demands, demands which she had neither invited nor wanted!

The blast of raging jealousy was as fast as it was furious.

'Of course you are.' His voice was thick with sexual gloating. 'Like me touching you there? What about if I do this?' He propelled her towards the padded window seat and she flung her head back with a wrenched cry of pleasure as he began to suckle on her nipple, drawing it into his mouth and teasing it with his tongue and his teeth. And her other breast was not free from his attention. No, he massaged that with his hand, making her squirm with shameless, wanton abandon.

The shirt trailed over her shoulders and her back was arched as she allowed her forbidden cravings to be satisfied. She half opened her eyes and watched, horribly turned on, his dark head at her breasts as he flicked his tongue on the sensitised tips.

There was something intensely masculine about his harsh, hungry love-making and, although it should have turned her off because she had always seen sex as something gentle and languorous, it perversely made her feel at her most feminine.

She *wanted* this big, powerful man on his knees before her, barely restraining himself as he lathered her breasts greedily with his mouth.

Her legs automatically parted and a soft noise, half sigh, half cry, escaped as he began pushing the skirt up, his hands traveling past her calves, past her knees until finally they were up around her thighs.

Every inch of her wanted this with a desperation that was

terrifying and, Lord knew, she would have gladly given herself to him had not the knock on the bedroom door catapulted them both out of their little private world and back into the reality they had left behind.

Pierre sprang to his feet and Georgie wasn't far behind, her fingers fumbling with the buttons of her blouse at precisely the same time as Didi poked her head round the door.

'Oops, sorry, darlings…' And she did sound very flustered. 'I interrupted you…'

'We were just…' Pierre glanced over his shoulder to Georgie, whose face was barely visible behind the tumble of blonde curls as she stared down at her feet '…about to come…' he left a fraction of a pause '…downstairs.'

'Take your time.' Didi was already closing the door and Georgie didn't feel she could actually draw breath until that door was quietly shut.

What had she been thinking? Had she lost her mind?

'This will never happen again,' she told him quietly. 'Never. Do you understand me?'

Pierre leaned against the wall and looked at her. Never? Was that a word that existed in his vocabulary? He inclined his head to one side, but didn't answer and, without a word Georgie swept past him, out of the bedroom, leaving him to think that there were certain things that sounded very much like a challenge to him and challenges, he would have been the first to admit, had always been his private obsession.

CHAPTER SIX

IT WAS after nine before Georgie managed to escape. Even then, it was amid a flurry of complaints from Didi, who didn't think that the Mini was anywhere near up to the job of delivering Georgie back to her house without developing some sort of terminal allergic reaction to the snow between Greengage Cottage and the village centre.

While Pierre looked at her thoughtfully from his position of superiority lounging against the kitchen sink with a dishcloth in one hand in an attempt to appear helpful, Didi did her best to persuade Georgie to hang on just for an hour or so and they could give her a lift back in the Bentley.

It had taken all her non-existent acting skills to turn down the offer while still managing to look as though nothing would have delighted her more, to edge towards the door without looking too desperate to get away.

But she had done it and now here she was, back in her own space and with the entire day to herself because Didi and Pierre were going on their shopping trip and wouldn't, thank the Lord, be back until late afternoon.

The snow had stopped falling and, although it was still freezing cold, the skies were a bright, unbroken blue and the sun was glittering, already melting the blanket of white that had looked so pretty earlier on. Georgie quietly prayed that the cold, fine weather would continue, which would mean that their meal out at one of the local restaurants could go ahead. In a threesome, there would be no chance of anything *getting out of control.*

When she thought about what had happened, she actually had to lean against something and close her eyes.

Not only had he *touched her*, but she had *wanted him to*, had virtually *begged* him by surrendering *all* attempts at self control. Had she even protested? She couldn't remember.

She threw herself into a frenzy of activity. She cleaned her house from top to bottom, which left her pleasantly exhausted by lunchtime, and then she began work on patching up the Santa Claus costume, which was in threads after years of use by old Mr Blackman, their regular Father Christmas who visited the kids at school and did his 'Ho, Ho, Ho' act, complete with sack of toys that the parents bought making sure that nothing was more expensive than a couple of pounds. He would be on display in a few days time and the white beard was beginning to look a lot worse for wear, like a rug that had been walked on too many times. With the telly blaring in the background, she could effectively lose herself in the minutiae of patching and darning and sprucing up.

Not that the images of Pierre touching her didn't penetrate the ferocity of her concentration. They did. His mouth at her breasts, his hands touching her, that glorious feeling of *wanting* to surrender to an unstoppable force. It had been like nothing she had ever felt before. Stan had been a gentle lover. Pierre, on the other hand, had overwhelmed her, turned her into a person she barely recognised.

She had been expecting to hear from Didi at some point and she did. At five-thirty her telephone rang and Didi, obviously on a high after a successful shopping trip with her son, barely sounded like the flat, lifeless woman she had been less than a fortnight ago. Her words were tripping over each other as she described the beautiful lunch they had had at one of the local hotels, the fantastic tea of fresh scones and clotted cream, the shops they had gone to in search of presents and Christmas tree decorations. Georgie tried to picture Pierre *shopping for presents and Christmas tree decorations* and found that she couldn't, although, really, thinking about it, her assumptions of him had been crumbling fast. How was *she* to know whether he adored tramping through shops before regaining his energy with a couple of hearty scones and cups of tea? Where were all those useful categories into which she had-pigeon holed him? Where was the good-looking but essentially boring, humourless, condescending workaholic? Nowhere much in evidence, thereby proving conclusively, she thought, that she was rubbish when it came to deciphering people and, more importantly, the opposite sex.

Furthermore, where was *she*? Where was the fun loving, good natured girl who had been so sure of being in control of the situation she had impulsively and foolishly generated? Where were all her reliable feelings of healthy antagonism towards him? She certainly hadn't been feeling too antagonistic that morning as she had succumbed to the massive sexual power she had never suspected him of having.

'The weather has cleared up beautifully.' Didi was now chattering merrily away. 'So we thought we'd go to Chez Zola as planned. Terribly formal compared to yesterday, I know, and if you'd rather we just stayed in—'

'No!' Even in the safety of her home, Georgie could feel nervous, prickly perspiration break out and she cleared her throat before continuing. 'No, I think it would be nice for us all to have a meal out. I'm dying to hear all about your day…it's been such a long time since you've ventured out shopping, Didi…' And this, she reminded herself, was what it was all about: Didi recapturing that spark that had disappeared from her life over the past few months.

'Oh, you don't want to hear me going on, Georgie…'

Georgie, with a sinking heart, detected something of a girlish giggle. 'Of course I do!' she said brightly. 'Pierre and I can…can always catch up…um…later…'

'Of course you can! Well…' Georgie heard her ask Pierre for timings and she shivered at the deep timbre of his voice as he indistinctly said something in the background, then Didi was back on the line, 'we'll pop across for you at about seven. A little early, but no point risking more poor weather by being out too late!'

Georgie couldn't agree more. She wanted to be firmly tucked up in her own bed tonight.

Meal at seven. Surely it wasn't asking too much to be back home and shutting her front door by ten?

With that optimistic thought in mind, she dressed, unusually for her, in something more sophisticated than she was accustomed to wearing. Actually, the only sophisticated outfit in her wardrobe. A long-sleeved, figure-hugging dress in deep burgundy and, instead of her usual flat, sensible, weatherproof Doc Martins, a pair of high heels, which might not be practical for the weather but were certainly essential Chez Zola footwear. She had never been to the restaurant, but she had heard enough about it to know that the casual look would not go down a storm.

'Nice outfit,' Pierre said as she opened the door to him and began sticking on her black coat. 'Shame about the woolly hat.'

'I don't intend to wear it in the restaurant,' Georgie snapped.

She had braced herself for seeing him but was still, idiotically, taken aback by how supremely sexy he looked, dark coat casually flapping open to reveal a crisp white shirt and dark trousers. Every bit of her felt horribly *alive* and alert to his presence, a fact she disguised under a scowl as she defensively yanked the woolly hat a bit lower.

'And you're wearing shoes.'

'I usually do!'

'Of a workmanlike variety.'

'Yes, well, they happen to be very useful in my kind of career! It's not practical to do playground duty in a pair of kitten heels!'

'Now, now,' Pierre chided. 'Snapping isn't very romantic behaviour with your lover, is it?'

He had spent a surprisingly restful day in the company of his mother. Having never been shopping with her before, or at least as far back as he could remember, he had not, over the passing years, noticed how much more tentative she was on her feet, relying on holding onto his arm as they ambled along the high street. Her spirits were high but her physical capabilities were more limited than he had expected and perhaps it was the arm-in-arm contact, but they had actually communicated without any formality or restraint.

He had not once glanced at his watch and wondered what was happening at the office, nor had he insisted on taking calls on his mobile because the cutthroat world of business, as he had often been wont to explain to her, didn't take time off when he happened to.

All in all he was feeling on top of the world.

'You're *not* my lover,' Georgie muttered, bristling and pink-cheeked.

Not yet, Pierre caught himself thinking and he smiled to himself. This morning had been something of a revelation for him. The awkward tomboy who had matured into the thoroughly irritating woman had been neither tomboy-ish nor irritating. And she had wanted him. Never mind her protests to the contrary.

'Oh, but we wouldn't want Didi to suspect that, would we?' He slipped his arm around her waist and got the distinct impression that she would have slapped it away if only she could have got away with it. As it was, he ushered her to the waiting Bentley, opening the door for her and slamming it shut once she was safely inside.

They had had a marvellous day, lots of shopping. Didi was in top form as they drove to the restaurant and she looked it as well, her cheeks pink, her eyes lively, and she had taken an awful lot of trouble with her clothes. It was a joy to see. She was wearing her favourite deep green checked skirt and a dark green jumper, which, she confided to Georgie as Pierre went ahead of them to chat to the manager, Pierre had insisted on buying for her.

'So he should,' Georgie said, trying to look the enchanted lover through gritted teeth and refraining from mentioning that he had precious little else on which to spend the vast amounts of money at his disposal.

'I know,' Didi agreed wistfully, 'but he never has. Not unless it's been a special occasion. Oh, yes, he's never forgotten a birthday or a Mother's Day, but this is the first time he's ever spontaneously bought something for me. I can't begin to tell you what that means. Must be love.'

'Of course he loves you.'

'No, darling, it must be because he's *in love*.'

Georgie was spared having to meet that statement with something suitably obscure by Pierre's return. A fair few of the diners had cancelled their reservations because of the weather, and they were shown to the best table in the house, nestled in an intimate corner where the black and white signed photographs on the walls reminded them that the restaurant had been visited by a host of celebrities down the years.

Georgie, especially when she managed to keep her eyes

firmly focused on Didi rather than on the man sitting to the right of her, looked forward to an evening of relative relaxation.

At least with Didi on the scene, the conversation wouldn't get too personal. Nothing, at any rate, that she couldn't handle and because the circular table was big Pierre was, thankfully, too far away for any of those loving gestures he seemed to think were of vital importance.

And tomorrow he would be gone. Back to London where they could conduct their love affair with the safety of several hundred miles between them. Conduct it and also work out how to jettison it before Didi got it into her head that the sound of church bells would be the next logical step in the scenario.

Her relief was short-lived. No sooner than pleasantries had been made about the menu, the choice of food and the wine selection, Pierre sat back in his chair and said, a little too carelessly for Georgie's liking, 'A man could get used to the open spaces. Quite a change from London…'

Georgie's antennae were immediately on full alert even though the observation was innocuous enough.

'I never thought I'd hear you say that, Pierre,' Didi told him, surprised.

'And I never thought I would,' he confessed. 'Maybe age is beginning to take its toll.' He gave Georgie a lazy half-smile. 'What do *you* think?'

'Oh, you're a city gent through and through!' She smiled ruefully at Didi and began to formulate the foundations for their eventual break-up. 'You know you've always wanted to live in London! You said so yourself! All that stuff about the cut and thrust of city life. I guess it's the excitement, the challenges…quite an addiction, I would say. So, you *might* think you like the peace of rural life but really, you'd be lost without London. Lots of people find that. They sell up and move to the country because they've been there a couple of times and they imagine that there couldn't be anything better than waking up to the sound of birds and farm animals. Then they get here and realise that there's no café lattes and baguettes within walking distance and no nightclubs to speak of and no sprawling choice of stage musicals on a Saturday evening... funny the things you get used to without even realising.' She looked ruefully at Didi. 'This is one of the many drawbacks of a long distance relationship.'

'You hardly live on opposite ends of the earth!' Didi exclaimed.

'I know, but, well, it's *more than that*, isn't it, Pierre?' She looked to Pierre for support, but he was frowning slightly, which made Georgie wonder whether she wasn't laying it on a bit thick. The last thing she wanted to do was alarm Didi, make her retreat back to that dark place from which she had just emerged.

'Is it?' Pierre asked mildly.

'Well, yes...of course it is!' She heard herself beginning to splutter and drew in a deep, steadying breath. Why on earth wasn't he supporting her? He had been dragged kicking and screaming into this situation and here she was, giving him the golden opportunity to begin opening his exit door, and what was he doing? Relaxing indolently back in his chair, head politely tilted to one side, looking at her as though she had suddenly begun speaking in tongues. Did he really not follow what she was trying to do? Or maybe, and this seemed a lot more likely, he was happy to let her flounder in her own confused, tentative outpourings, thereby allowing himself the privilege of being able to turn around at a later date and say to Didi, *Well, I was willing to give it a go, but Georgie...*

'What do you mean, darling?' Didi was beginning to look perplexed.

'Oh, nothing really. I was just saying how awkward it can

be trying to unite different backgrounds...' Lord, now she was beginning to sound as though she came from a different planet.

'It's easy to let small pitfalls turn into insurmountable obstacles,' Didi said thoughtfully, 'but sometimes the pitfalls are what make us stronger people...sometimes they can cement love into something truly lasting and unshakeable...'

Georgie grunted. Out of the corner of her eye she could see a waiter approaching them, thank heavens. She crossed her fingers and hoped that the temporary diversion as they ordered food would rescue her, but as soon as the wine was poured and the waiter had disappeared Didi returned to the conversation, waxing lyrical now about the compromises needed for a relationship to survive and the shocking ease with which young people seemed to get married only to divorce a few years later, as though the marriage contract were little more than a piece of paper that could be chucked in the fire the minute the going got tough.

Georgie now felt almost as if she were one of those paper-chucking-into-fire people, while Pierre, sipping his wine, was somehow pure as the driven snow. She gulped down a generous mouthful of wine and clenched her fists on her lap, safely out of sight underneath the starched white linen tablecloth.

'I agree—' she struggled to bring things back on track '—absolutely. It's just that Pierre is so...' she gave him a smile and hoped it summed up exactly how she was feeling '...*exciting* and *ambitious* and *well travelled*. I just worry, *darling*, that you won't get bored with little ole me...' She reached out and gave his hand a little squeeze and then left it there, with her nails digging into his palm. Typically the gesture backfired as he brought her hand to his lips and gently kissed her fingers, every inch the besotted lover who clearly had no idea why she was making such a deal of something as insignificant as a few miles.

'I'm flattered that you find me so fascinating,' he murmured tweaking her description just that bit so that he was elevated a couple of notches. 'I assure you I could never find you boring.'

Georgie wriggled her hand, which he now firmly placed in his so that their linked hands were on the table, making a nonsense of her feeble suggestions that the miles between them, the vast difference of their personalities, were dramatic problems lurking in the wings, ready to pounce at any given moment, and Didi, ever the incurable romantic, had no trouble in falling for the phony gesture hook, line and sinker.

'The opposite,' Pierre murmured lovingly. 'Your every move is unpredictable. You're spontaneous and utterly impulsive. Wouldn't you agree? The times you've surprised me in London…showing up literally out of thin air! Prepared to do anything on the spur of the moment…' He stroked her hand with one of his fingers and it sent a red hot current shooting through her. 'Hardly the sort who could ever be boring!'

'Opposites *do* attract,' Didi mused thoughtfully.

'I hope you're not implying that *I'm* the boring half of this relationship, Didi!' Pierre laughed. 'Because if so, you're in a minority of one considering this hussy next to me finds me scintillating.'

Hussy? Was he referring to her behaviour that morning before? Making fun of her because she couldn't possibly defend herself with Didi sitting there, smiling contentedly at them?

'And so you are,' Didi agreed with an indulgent chuckle. 'What a shame you have to dash back up to London so soon. Just when…when…'

Georgie snatched her hand free. 'I know. Shame. But work calls! Perfectly understandable! I never understood the compulsion to work every hour of every day, but I certainly *have* learnt to respect that side of you, Pierre!' She turned to Didi. 'Compromise and all that!'

'And far too much of it!' Pierre returned, allowing a pregnant silence as the waiter placed starters in front of them.

'Which,' he announced with satisfaction, 'is why I have contacted my office and informed them that I will be taking the next week off! I did say that this country life's beginning to get to me. Do you know, it's been years since I had any kind of holiday from work? I think I deserve it. Especially when I have such temptations waiting here for me!'

Georgie couldn't help it. Her mouth dropped in sheer, horrified amazement.

'You *can't!*' she spluttered. 'I mean…don't you have that really big, really *important* deal thing going on? The one you told me about? Meetings…conferences…lawyers…'

'What deal thing?' Pierre asked, frowning. 'Be a bit more specific.'

'I can't remember the *exact* deal,' Georgie gritted, 'but you mentioned…you mentioned that you absolutely *had* to be in the office *Monday at the latest!*'

'Plans change.'

'That's wonderful news, Pierre!' Didi was pink with pleasure at this unexpected development.

'Honestly, Pierre!' Georgie tried to sound delighted. 'Don't forget that *I shall be working!* Seems silly to take time off when I'll be busy *virtually every minute of the day!*'

'And never you mind,' he soothed. 'I'll be working a fair bit of the time myself. I have my laptop with me! And there are one or two things around the house I want to see to.'

'Such as?' Georgie asked in a high voice.

'Small leak in the guest bathroom…a couple of cracks on walls need painting.'

'You don't do DIY, Pierre!'

'Maybe I've decided to start.' He smiled at her, challenging her to carry on until she had well and truly boxed herself in. 'Darling.'

'Better late than never,' Didi said stoutly. 'Doing your own odd jobs can be very satisfying and I won't deny that it'll be wonderful having a man around the house. It's been such a long time.'

Georgie wished that she could be a little more magnanimous on Didi's behalf, but her nerves had been everywhere since Pierre had descended on them and she had been looking forward to his departure with something bordering on desperation.

'And we can always meet up in the evenings, or rather the pair of you can! I'm just as happy to catch up on my reading. Have I mentioned, darling, that I've started back with my book club? My, this food was delicious!'

'How long do you plan on sticking around?' Georgie was hardly aware of Didi in the background.

'Not sure.' He raised his eyebrows and grinned. 'Maybe some of your impulsiveness is beginning to rub off on me.'

Georgie, defeated, could barely enjoy the exquisite food that was put in front of her. Why was he doing this?

She found that she was willing the evening to end, and not because she wanted to get back home, though she did, but more importantly she wanted to find out just what the hell he thought he was doing.

And there seemed little likelihood of her questions being answered as she was dropped off first, her house being on the way, and Pierre saw her to the door, only telling her *en route* that, for someone who prided herself on being carefree and fun-loving, she certainly looked as though she was about to explode.

'I am!'

'Bad for the blood pressure,' he whispered, and while she was still glaring and thinking of a suitable comeback he bent and kissed her swiftly on the lips, not giving her time to pull away.

And *that* was why she had wanted him gone. Because that fleeting touch of his mouth against hers touched the very core of her, touched her almost as powerfully as if he had made love to her. She seemed to have no protective layer against that, no defences that were sturdy enough to hold him at bay.

And she had another week of him! Hanging around! Playing the good lover whenever Didi was around! How on earth was she going to cope? How many excuses could she rummage up for avoiding him without Didi smelling a rat? Her innocent and naïve belief that this charade would bring the desired results, no harm done, was in mortal danger of becoming the most hideous piece of misjudgement she had ever made in her entire life.

And she still had to talk to Pierre!

Her head was spinning by the time she was in her pyjamas. The doorbell rang five times before Georgie, cocooned in her bedroom in front of a book and with the small, portable radio as background noise, was even aware of a visitor. Furthermore she knew exactly who it would be and decided that she wasn't in the mood to have a conversation with him. Not when she was in her pyjamas and still seething. Tomorrow, she would be calm and controlled and would be able to handle him like an adult. She switched off the bedroom light, buried her head under the pillow so that she couldn't hear the doorbell, and grinned at the thought of him stamping his feet outside her front door in the freezing cold, not, for once, getting his own way.

She was unaware of the soft pad of footsteps up her staircase as Pierre tentatively pushed open doors on the landing until he found her bedroom.

He switched on the overhead light and watched as the buried lump under the quilt yelped and eventually emerged, hair everywhere and green eyes spitting fury.

'I *did* ring the doorbell,' he said, bypassing pleasantries.

'How did you get in?'

'Key.' He jangled his trouser pocket provocatively. 'Didi has a spare on a hook by the Aga.'

'So you just *took it and headed over*!'

'That's about the size of it.' He stepped into the bedroom, which was cluttered but not in an unpleasant manner. The dress she had worn earlier hung over the chair by the dressing table and several outfits, which he suspected she might have earlier tried on, were piled randomly on the weathered pine trunk by the bay window. Here was someone who had no hang-ups about neatness. A scented candle had obviously been burning because the room smelt of sandalwood and he thought that a nice touch. 'Actually Didi was surprised I didn't have my own key, but I told her that you always travelled up to London to see me.' She had now wriggled into a semi-sitting position and folded her arms protectively. 'You spent the entire evening fulminating. Why?'

'This is neither the time nor the pla—'

'Yes, yes, yes. And now we've established that, are you going to spit it out?' He strolled across to the bay window, shoved aside the pile of clothes and sat down, stretching out his long legs and relaxing back to stare at her. He doubted she knew what a fierce turn-on she was, with her rumpled vanilla-blonde hair and her angry green eyes. He doubted she was aware of how those angry green eyes would slide furtively towards him, fascinated and caressing and guilty all at once. He had done his own fair share of furtive watching over dinner…little did she know, but watching her watching him had been an erotic little game.

Ever since that morning, she had been playing games with him, keeping him at arm's length when those hot eyes were begging him to get closer. Who was he to resist the pull of Nature?

He hadn't anticipated being attracted to the woman. It was

a complication which, he had to admit, was proving intensely enjoyable. Those Keep Out signs she was plastering all around her were a nuisance, however.

'We could always go downstairs if you find it awkward being in bed…'

Georgie thought of him sitting there, watching her as she clambered out from under the duvet in her unappealing nightwear. 'Okay. I'll say what I have to say and then I want you to leave. Understood?'

'Sure.'

'What do you think you were playing at this evening?'

Pierre frowned and crossed his legs. Just looking at her was beginning to arouse him! It was crazy. He stood up and began pacing the small room, to distract himself from the way she was leaning forward, affording him a tantalising glimpse of those soft, small breasts.

'Explain.'

'Don't pretend, Pierre! You know exactly what I'm talking about! I gave you the perfect opportunity for us to start finding a way out of this relationship!'

'Oh, yes, it's coming back to me now.' He stopped pacing and stood at the foot of the bed, six feet two inches of pure, sinfully sexy male. When he rested his hands on the foot stead and leaned forward, Georgie unconsciously shifted back. 'I was supposed to agree to being a workaholic, someone who couldn't possibly live without…what was it? Oh, yes, *the cut and thrust of city life*, the sort of single minded bore who couldn't sustain a relationship in a hundred years.'

'I never said that you were a *bore*,' Georgie contradicted sulkily.

'Oh, forgot. I was exciting and ambitious and well-travelled. So exciting and ambitious and well-travelled that anything rural couldn't fail to bring on rapid mental shutdown.'

'There's nothing wrong with that,' Georgie said defensively. 'You must have been able to see what I was doing?'

'Must I?'

'Yes! Laying the foundations! Your life in London…me down here…what better way to at least start bracing Didi for the eventuality that the distance and the *differences* between us would get in the way?'

Pierre nodded thoughtfully and strolled to the side of the bed and sat down. Georgie looked at him warily. 'You mean you agree? I thought you might! I mean, it makes sense, doesn't it? You could even *go away*!'

'Anywhere in particular?'

'China! That's a developing country with a growing economy! Isn't it? You could go to China to…to…do whatever it is you do…oversee an important deal…'

'And for how long?' Pierre asked with interest.

'A few months? A year? Two years? What relationship could withstand that length of separation? Of course I would pine but eventually I would carry on…'

'Hurt…disillusioned…wounded, but not mortally… I, on the other hand, would presumably return once every six months, ruthlessly moving forward with my empire-building, and naturally we would avoid one another like the plague because of water under the bridge.'

'Yes!'

'Personally, I don't much care for the thought of China.'

'Well, you could vanish somewhere else,' Georgie said irritably.

'I don't like the thought of *vanishing*, period. I happen to be rather enjoying the country life, as a matter of fact. I intend on coming here *more often* rather than less. No…I have a better idea, Georgina…'

Georgie swallowed and said on a whisper, 'What?'

'I think,' Pierre told her softly, 'that we need to look at the situation from a completely different standpoint. Here we are...pretending to be lovers when there's no need for the pretence.' His blue eyes, she thought, were mesmerising, and his voice, low and velvety, seemed to be dragging her down. 'I'm not going to lie to you...I want you and I know the feeling's mutual...'

Georgie opened her mouth to protest and he raised one finger and gently held back the denial.

'So...' he shrugged '...why fight it? No need for you to scuttle away whenever I come near you. I *want* to touch you and *you* want to touch me back.'

Like a predator, he had sensed her weakness and was moving in for the kill. Emotion didn't enter his equations. They wanted each other and enough said. Like animals obeying instinct without thought.

A tidal wave of shame washed over Georgie, giving her the strength to look at him coldly.

'That's such an enticing thought, Pierre. Really, though, I'm going to have to turn you down.'

'Why?' He raked his fingers through his hair, perplexed.

'We've discussed this before.'

'Yes, *before* this attraction sprang up between us.'

'And I don't believe in a romp in the sack. It doesn't matter if there's a mutual attraction or not—you're responsible for your own morality, Pierre, and I'm responsible for mine.'

'Oh, for God's sake! We're not talking about burning down the local school, Georgie! We're talking about having fun.' Had he *ever* been turned down in his life before? '*Permitted* fun, incidentally.'

'You're forgetting what this is. Just one big *act* and I'm not something convenient that you can take because you want it. I guess now that your girlfriend is no longer on the scene you think that I might be an amusing plaything while you're here, and what's the big deal?'

'I didn't hear you objecting this morning… If Didi hadn't walked in on us, we probably wouldn't be having this conversation right now at all. In fact, we would probably be lying in this bed making love…'

Georgie liked to imagine that she would have found the energy to pull back *whatever*. 'I don't know how that happened…'

'I touched you and you went up in flames. *That's* how it happened.' He was on losing ground. Unbelievable! What century did this woman live in? 'It's called having fun. Sitting around waiting for Mr Right is called *wasting time*.'

'It's called *shoving my principles on the back-burner*. And sitting around *waiting for Mr Right,* which, incidentally, is *not* what I'm doing, is called *believing in love*. You're a cynic, Pierre.'

'And you, my darling, are a hypocrite.' He walked towards the door and lounged against it for a few seconds. 'But…' he shrugged '…your choice.' He could feel his male pride slam into place. 'Word of warning, though…self-denial might be morally noble, but when you're shivering in your celibate bed it doesn't make a very warming companion.'

Typically, every clever retort to that stunningly arrogant observation, and there were a fair few, sprang to mind roughly ten minutes after he had left the room.

At which point the most she could do was dredge up memories of why she disliked him and remind herself that he was nothing but a self-centred, high-handed, unprincipled pig!

CHAPTER SEVEN

GEORGIE half hoped that Pierre would do her the enormous favour of finding an excuse to leave earlier than he had planned and it took every ounce of her charitable nature to remind herself that Didi was enjoying every second of having her son with her, even if *she* could think of nothing worse.

At least, however, there was work on Monday and even Didi didn't harbour unrealistic expectations that Georgie would take time off work because Pierre just happened to be around. She knew how much Georgie's teaching job meant to her. Far and beyond the basic need to pay bills and keep a roof over her head, Georgie derived a great deal of pleasure from her motley crew of children. Having neither parents nor siblings and with no children of her own, she considered her pupils at the local primary school more than just little people she taught because she was obliged to. She spent a great deal of unpaid overtime preparing lessons that were just that little bit different, supervising after-school events that most of the other teachers tried to avoid, especially in winter, and as Christmas approached was in charge of all things to do with the school play and the much awaited visit from Santa.

Right now, she was inordinately grateful for the distraction of her job. In fact, she was the first to arrive at the school. Any earlier and she reckoned that she might well be passing Jim, the night watchman, on his way out. But she hadn't been able to sleep.

Pierre's words kept playing in her head, like a needle stuck in a groove, repeating over and over *why fight it, why fight it, why fight it…?*

She had wasted a lot of beauty sleep primly telling herself that she had been *absolutely right* to have reacted the way that she had, that it was typical of a man whose ego was the size of a house to just *assume* that he could have whatever he wanted, including *her*.

Admittedly, she *had* given him signs that she was attracted to him, but as she had tossed and turned towards dawn she felt quietly pleased with herself for having informed him in no uncertain terms that she was stronger than any passing attraction that might have temporarily laid waste to her will-power.

By six in the morning, she had exhausted her imaginative repertoire of scenarios in which she was the proud bearer of morality and sense of principle, stating her case in loud, ringing tones while he listened, awestruck and, best of all, *admitted* that she was right and he was wrong, that he respected her point of view and admired her for standing up for her beliefs.

When she thought of his hands exploring her and that seductive voice of his telling her not to resist him, that she could have more of what she wanted, she immediately filled her head with other, more helpful things. Such as eighteen little children who still needed to get through a little bit of work while the promise of Christmas threatened to have them running out of control.

She planned on making sure that when she went across to Didi's after work, much later than she promised with some vague excuse about *work,* she would be able to actually look Pierre in the eye and feel secure on her own moral high ground.

The words had an unfortunate ring. They reminded her of criticisms he had made to her in the past, criticisms of being prissy and judgemental.

Georgie told herself that essentially there was nothing wrong with that because it was far better to have *some* moral guidelines, rather than end up like Pierre, emotionally adrift, finding passing pleasure in women with whom he had no spiritual connection and who would sail out of his life without leaving much of a mark behind them. Now *that*, she told herself, was *sad*.

She was still stoutly telling herself that as she got dressed later that evening. Nothing fancy this time. Didi was cooking a meal and Georgie had no intention of dressing up because she didn't want Pierre to think that she was making a special effort on his behalf.

She tied her hair back into two wispy pigtails, and back she was in her usual garb of flowing skirt, flat boots and an array of tops, which started with her two layers of jumpers and culminated in her wraparound poncho, which was vibrant and very, very warm but would have had any well-groomed sophisticate reaching for her designer suite jacket.

In summer she would have thought nothing of hopping onto her bike but, although the snow had stopped, temperatures were freezing and it was miserable outside.

Much as she wanted to dawdle, arriving an hour and a half late with potential frostbite because she had cycled was not an option. She drove. But she did her damnedest not to think of Pierre on the way. She had problems with Santa and thinking about that was restful in comparison.

She arrived to find an anxious Didi with her hand virtually on the doorknob, waiting for her to arrive.

'Where have you been, my darling?' A kiss on either cold cheek, accompanied by a worried frown. 'We were *so* worried! We tried to call, but there was no answer! Do you know, Pierre was about to come searching for you!'

Georgie guiltily thought of the phone ringing as she lay in the bath, slowly shrivelling from staying there way too long.

'I'm sorry, Didi. Work. Usual Christmas problems…you look lovely! Don't tell me you've got *another* new jumper!'

'A few, actually! Pierre's just through in the kitchen. Very informal tonight. Just a casserole.'

Georgie stripped off her poncho and one of the jumpers, leaving just a fitted thin woolen jumper and her long skirt. 'I've dressed for the occasion,' she joked, but her stomach was doing its usual somersaults as they strolled, still chatting, into the kitchen. Even her breasts were weirdly tingling, as if her body had gone onto red alert and was reacting accordingly.

Pierre, with his back to her, was stirring the ubiquitous pot that had filled the kitchen with a wonderful aroma. The pine table was already set for three and Georgie felt another twinge of guilt at her late arrival. She should have been there forty five minutes ago.

'Smells yummy,' she said, reluctantly walking towards Pierre because that was what would be expected. He turned around and this time the grin on Georgie's face was genuine.

'Goodness, Pierre! *You're wearing an apron.*' She took a couple of steps back and looked at him critically. 'Golly, I wish I'd brought my camera!' She started laughing. The apron was one she had bought for Didi years back on the spur of the moment and it sported an amusing little saying about women never divorcing men who wore aprons. 'Don't tell me *you've cooked!*' she spluttered, trying to swallow down the laughter because those blue, blue eyes didn't seem to be sharing her level of amusement.

'It's not unheard of,' Pierre muttered, scowling. She came

in, looking like a teenager with those blonde pigtails, her cheeks still pink from the cold outside…laughing so that her face softened…making inroads into his pride, which had slammed into place the minute she had refused his advances. *Refused him!*

'Unheard of for *you*!' Georgie laughed, throwing her head back.

'Fair enough,' Pierre muttered, exerting undue force as he spun around and begin vigorously stirring the contents of the big pan. Aware of Didi busying herself as she poured Georgie a glass of wine, Pierre forced himself to relax. 'Anyone can follow instructions from a recipe book,' he said, very much aware of her peering curiously into the pot as though suspicious of its contents.

'Have you ever?'

'No.'

'Bet you don't even own a recipe book!' Georgie hooted.

'Which,' Didi piped up, 'is a very good idea for a Christmas present.'

That made Georgie stop in her tracks. Christmas. Of course, she was *supposed* to buy him a Christmas present! It was to be expected.

'Oh, we've decided not to give each other any Christmas presents,' Pierre said smoothly, and even though he had beat her to an excuse Georgie still felt an unwelcome little surge of hurt.

'What on earth do you mean?' Didi sounded perplexed.

'We thought…' Georgie said, thinking on her feet, 'we just thought…that it might be nicer to *donate* the money to one of the homeless shelters. There are so many people who have absolutely nothing and Christmas is such a wonderful opportunity for us to just…play our part…'

'That's a lovely sentiment, darling…' Didi handed her a

glass of wine and smiled. 'Although Pierre already does so much for the underprivileged.'

'He does?' Georgie looked at him. 'You do?'

'I've only found out myself today, haven't I, Pierre?' She smiled warmly at her son's back as he continued to stir a concoction that no longer needed stirring. 'We popped into St Michael's Church to get some charity Christmas cards and one of the ladies in charge of the stall recognised him. Didn't she, Pierre? I'm surprised he hasn't told you himself!'

Surprise wasn't the word Georgie would have used to describe how she was feeling. More dumbstruck. 'P-probably his natural modesty,' she managed to stutter. 'You never said you—'

'I know. Shocking, isn't it?' Pierre leant towards her, out of range of his mother's eagle ears—she might be a little slower on her pegs but there was nothing wrong with her hearing. 'I'm not the complete bastard you think I am.'

'Pierre has set up a fund through his company which helps with urban regeneration and, as a part of that, helps displaced teenagers to find creative outlets. Christmas-card designing is just one of the things and the lady in question had brought several packs down to sell as she's here for the holiday to stay with her daughter…'

Georgie felt unreasonably miffed that that little snippet of information about him had managed to creep under her skin so that it could niggle away at her defences. She pasted a smile on her face and left him to his pot.

After that, what was there to say?

The meal, when finally brought to the table by a man who waved down both their offers of help, was as good as it had smelled. And, Georgie noticed, there were no superfluous loving asides as accompaniment. She was irked to find herself disappointed by the lack of teasing familiarity with which she

ad become familiar, even if only in the sense that she slapped
t away whenever she could. He was, as far as Didi was con-
erned, just the same as ever, but *she* noticed the difference.
He no longer brushed against her, or watched her through
hose amazing eyes of his, as if drinking her in even when he
ould see that she was plainly irritated by the interest.

He had got the message about her once and for all, and for
hat, she decided, she should be well and truly thankful.
Wasn't it what she had wanted?

In fact, he barely looked at her, although his lack of interest
wasn't obvious. There were no lulls in the conversation, which
would have pointed to an underlying tension. Rather, he was
as relaxed and charming as she had ever seen him. She just
ensed the change.

'Maybe I'll get around to doing a bit more of this culinary
tuff,' he said, when his meal had been duly complimented.

'Things will change when you're back in your natural
abitat,' Georgie said darkly, and this time he *did* spare her
he briefest of looks.

'You're probably right,' he agreed, standing up so that he
ould complete his perfect pretence of being a domesticated
reature by taking the dishes to the sink. 'A leopard never
hanges its spots, does it, Georgina? We may think we're free
o do what we want, but the reality of it is that we're stuck in
ur ways, unwilling or unable to ever break free.'

'That's very deep, Pierre.' Didi laughed.

Georgie blushed and looked away. 'That's right,' she said
n a high voice. 'I mean, do you really think you'll ever cook
a meal when you get back to London? At the end of the week?'

'Depends on the woman…'

Didi, mistakenly, assumed that he was referring to Georgie.
Georgie knew better. This was his way of telling her that the
ea was very full of fish.

'Darling.' Didi interrupted and Georgie wondered if her antennae had picked up the awkward undercurrent, 'you were saying something about work…'

'Was I?'

'Isn't that why you were late?'

'Oh, yes! Course! Work! You know how it is, Didi…Christmas around the corner and as usual half the stuff has either gone missing in action or else been attacked by moths.'

'What stuff?' Pierre sauntered towards the kitchen table and sat down, hooking his foot under a chair so that he could drag it closer to him as a makeshift footrest.

'Nothing interesting. Honestly, Pierre, you'd find it very dull.'

'Oh, yes, forgot, I'm a high powered city guy who's kidding himself that he can ever enjoy the rural life…

'I'm seriously tempted,' he murmured, folding his hands behind his head and staring at her through half-closed eyes, 'to issue you with a little bet.'

'What's that?'

'It's easy to sit there and talk about people not being able to adapt to different surroundings, yet I know you don't speak from experience…'

'What do you mean?' Georgie asked faintly, not liking the sound of where this was going.

'You don't *know* about whether I could grow to enjoy the simple life any more than you know whether *you* could enjoy the city life. In actual fact, I'm more qualified than you are on the subject because I've experienced both…you, on the other hand, have not…'

'That's a silly bet.' Georgie looked to Didi for support, but was alarmed to see the older woman nodding thoughtfully and tugging on her earring.

'Pierre's got a point,' Didi said slowly. 'You've never really experienced much of a city life, have you, Georgie? I mean, you grew up around here and, yes, there was your university stint, but still a university in the country…hmm…'

'I've always enjoyed living in the country,' Georgie said in a measured voice, eyes averted from Pierre. 'Some people do.'

'But it might be rather nice for you to experience life in the fast lane,' Didi commented. 'The shops, the restaurants, the theatres…all the excitement…'

Georgie looked at Pierre accusingly. Now even Didi was on his side. She wanted to stamp her feet and throw a tantrum. 'Maybe you're right,' she said demurely. 'But while we're on the subject of alternative experiences, I have one that's a little closer to home for you, Pierre.'

'Oh?'

'Yup.' She flashed him a look that he, personally, considered pretty seductive. Or was his mind playing tricks on him? He frowned sternly back at her.

'It's Santa,' she said airily.

'Santa. No idea what you're on about, but, then again, it won't be the first time I've found myself in that particular boat with you.'

'Remember I was saying what a hectic day it'd been at school today? Well, part of the headache has been that Mr Blackman, who usually does his Santa routine for the kids, is in hospital. Slipped on a patch of icy road and sprained his ankle rather badly.'

'Oh, no!' Pierre was beginning to get the picture. 'No way.'

'What about all this stuff about challenges?' Georgie smiled smugly. 'I'm just challenging you to do something very small, Pierre. Honestly. A couple of hours out of your day. Surely you can spare that?'

'I can't imagine you in a Santa outfit,' Didi remarked, looking very much as if she would love to see it. 'Your dad used to dress up as Santa every year until you were about seven. Then you stopped believing in Santa, but, oh, how you loved it!'

'I don't remember that,' Pierre said, momentarily distracted. At the back of his mind, a memory tugged. 'Anyway—' back to the present '—it's out of the question.'

'Why? It would be such a help, Pierre.'

'What about one of the fathers? Surely there must be a dad or two from the school who wouldn't mind stepping in to fill the gap? Someone who would be a hell of a lot more credible than I ever could be.'

'Nope. Can't think of one.' *Could think of dozens.*

'I'm not the right shape and there's not enough time to fatten me up.'

'Oh, don't worry about that! You'd be amazed what a bit of padding can do! A cushion here…a cushion there…'

'I'll leave you two to fight it out, shall I?' Didi yawned. 'I'm going to head upstairs. Watch a little telly, I think. There's that excellent drama on in half an hour. But, Pierre—' she looked at him firmly '—I think you should take up Georgie's challenge. Just think of all those little smiling faces.'

As soon as she had vanished from the kitchen Pierre looked at Georgie with a scowl. 'You have my mother to thank for this.'

'So you agree?'

'Reluctantly.'

'It's just a little singsong, a few Christmas Carols at the school and then you can give out the presents.'

'And what do you do for me in return?'

Georgie felt her heart skip a beat, but the gaze she gave him was uncomprehending.

'Meaning?'

'Try some city life. Even Didi agrees with me. I'm not talking about London. That might be a little daunting for the uninitiated.'

'Teaching jobs aren't that easy to find! And for your information, I could easily do London!'

'Oh, really.'

'I've got to head back, Pierre.' She stood up and he followed her out into the hall, watching as she slung on her colourful layers, ending with the ever-hardy poncho. He had never liked her style of dressing. For him, it had always epitomised the country bumpkin, stubbornly refusing to give in to fashion, as if there were something irresponsible about looking glamorous. He didn't seem to mind it now. It was unique and quirky and weirdly feminine. Ultra feminine.

'I'll drive you,' he said brusquely, looking away, and, as expected, she launched into an immediate protest. She could drive back herself, thank you very much...she *had* after all, been driving quite merrily in the depths of winter before he came along...she had her mobile and obviously if her car decided to bite the dust mid route then she would give him a call and he could rescue her...

Pierre shrugged. 'Suit yourself. I'm going to London for the day tomorrow but I'll be back mid-morning on Wednesday. What time do you want me to show up?'

'Two would be great. I...I'll bring the costume into school tomorrow...that's usually the routine. The sack of presents is already locked away in the staff room and you can change there. Is that okay?' She turned away, heading for the door. Now that Didi was no longer on the scene, all semblance of politeness had been dropped and his indifference got to her. With one hand on the doorknob, she turned to him and said, jerkily, 'What Didi said about...your charity work... I had no idea and I want you to know that I think it's brilliant. Marvellous.' She met his eyes squarely and Pierre fought down an irrational urge to mentally preen and pat himself on the back.

'Never judge a book by its cover. I'll see you day after tomorrow.' He reached and pulled open the door. The blast of cold air reminded her that he wanted her gone. No need for pretence and certainly no need to try and sweeten her up with lots of empty, pretty words, not now that she had informed him where she stood when it came to any sexual involvement between them.

Georgie, even though she had come to recognise his dependability, still wasn't completely sure that he would return to Devon from London. He would for Didi, but then he might very well try and persuade her to join him in London for a couple of days. He had been staging a low level attack over the past few days, using all the charm at his disposal, not to mention their rapprochement, to convince her that London was not all about concrete buildings, crowds and high levels of pollution. Like Georgie, she was immune to the carrot of great shopping and Pierre had wisely jettisoned that line of argument before it had had a chance to backfire.

Maybe Didi would be heading up to London and she, Georgie, would be safely ensconced down here, away from him, busy with her job and her silly Santa Claus traumas.

But no. A telephone call to Didi soon set her straight on that. Pierre was definitely coming back down and she was to pull out her finest clothes because he would be taking her out in the evening.

'And never fear, darling, I won't be playing gooseberry this time!'

When Georgie, thinking he might launch her *own* attack to getting Didi to join them for dinner, suggested dropping in with some quiche for lunch, she found her plans scuppered by a sprightly Didi who informed her that she was spending the day with some of her friends who had dropped off the radar during her slide into depression. Bridge and then tea in the village. She was just to *enjoy herself with Pierre;* they deserved it.

Georgie brooded that what they deserved, given the circumstances, certainly wasn't the unbridled innocent enjoyment Didi had in mind.

By the time mid-afternoon arrived, her nerves were at breaking-point, not helped by the kids who had worked themselves up into a frenzy of excitement. The Christmas singsong was for the benefit of the parents. From behind the curtains on the stage, Georgie could hear them gathering in the small assembly hall, then the scraping of chairs as they took their seats. They would be uncomfortable but the performance was a scant half an hour, after which they would leave and Santa, wherever he was because he certainly hadn't arrived as yet, would do the honours.

She listened to the concert from the wings, ever watchful for any child suddenly in desperate need of the toilet or casually deciding to have a walkabout, perhaps in the direction of camcorder wielding parents. Her anxiety at spending the evening alone with Pierre had lessened considerably in comparison to her anxiety at discovering that he hadn't shown up for his impromptu performance.

She need not have worried. The children were shepherded backstage, the parents were ushered out, and as she was re-arranging the hall with the help of two of the teachers she looked up to see him in the doorway and for a few seconds she stilled, one hand on the back of the chair. Then she gathered herself and went across to him. Naturally the room had stilled. All eyes were on him, because as Santa Clauses went, Pierre cut an unreasonably dashing one.

'Surprised to see me here?' he asked coolly, reading her expression. His remote, vaguely hostile tone of voice was offset by the red and white costume, however, and the silvery white beard that he was holding in one hand. It was an effort not to grin so she looked down briefly and then called over to her colleagues so that she could introduce him.

'You don't look very plausible,' she said, leading him in the direction of the staff room. 'When did you arrive?'

'Just in time to hear the final few bars of "Silent Night".'

'Beautiful, wasn't it?' Georgie couldn't quite bring herself to look at him. Yes, he was in a foul mood and probably cursing her under his breath, but to see the man who ruled the waves in a red outfit that was several sizes too big, clutching a white beard and wearing a pair of black boots in which he was in obvious discomfort as they were probably a couple of sizes too small, risked engendering an attack of nervous hysterics.

'This is ridiculous.'

'I know, but I really do appreciate the favour, Pierre. Look, I've got a couple of cushions in the store cupboard.' She produced two disreputable flowered cushions, which he gazed at in perfect, blank-faced bewilderment.

'What the hell am I supposed to do with these?'

'Haven't you ever been in fancy dress before?' Georgie asked innocently.

'Give them here.' He unbuttoned the shirt, scowling as he tried to stuff them in until finally she took the cushion and expertly slotted it inside the gaping top, then she patted the round, soft stomach and stood back to have a critical inspection.

'You're enjoying this, aren't you?'

'Everyone should do something ridiculous at least once in their life. Have you ever done something ridiculous, Pierre?'

'I can think of at least one thing.' And ridiculous didn't come close to describing it, he thought, not least because the woman had been on his mind every second of his day in London. If that wasn't the definition of a ridiculous situation, then what was?

'You'll need to stick the beard on as well,' Georgie said abruptly. She turned away and walked out of the room.

The younger classes were all assembled back in the hall and in their school uniforms and, from the hassled expressions on the teachers' faces, had not been little angels. Georgie clapped her hands and without looking around, announced, with suitable levels of excitement, that Father Christmas was now going to be entering the hall so they needed to now *shh*. Magically, they did, and from behind her came the sound of Pierre entering the room, his voice booming out as he played his part. He might have been a reluctant volunteer but Georgie had to take her hat off to him. He made an excellent Santa. Where old Mr Blackman had followed the traditional routine of calling the children up one by one to have a little chat before he handed over the present, Pierre shouted for them all to sit around him. Instant mayhem, but with that intangible cloak of authority that seemed to make people want to obey him, he held the thirty-odd children mesmerised. He was funny and chatty and gave a touching little speech about remembering the meaning of Christmas, for which he earned a hearty round of applause.

Afterwards, pupils safely out of the building, he was surrounded by the teachers. The female ones, Georgie was disgusted to note, had begun to titter as he pulled off the beard and stepped out of the outfit, under which he was wearing a pair of faded denim jeans and a short-sleeved white tee shirt that made him look even more dangerously sexy.

She hovered on the sidelines, observing the effect he had on the women. Oh, good grief! Was *she* like that? They were positively drooling! Even Mrs Evans, who was at least sixty and a grandmother!

'I'm going to head off now,' she said awkwardly. 'Janice, will you make sure to lock up?' Had anyone even heard her? A lone voice emerged, telling her that that was fine and see her in the morning. She swore she also heard someone giggle something about *hunk*. Huh!

And she had to face an uncomfortable dinner with the man who now had zero to say to her and would probably yawn his way through the meal until he could decently leave.

He would be passing by for her at seven. Georgie knew this because she had phoned Didi only to discover that Pierre had not yet returned. Nearly six in the evening and where was he? She felt a rush of jealousy tear through her and she had to grit her teeth through Didi's perfectly jolly conversation, which concluded with telling her that her date would be swinging by at seven and, not meaning to spoil the surprise, but they would be going to that smart new fish restaurant that had opened up in the city.

'Does that mean my wardrobe won't make the grade?' Georgie joked.

'Don't be silly!' Didi was horrified. 'Darling girl, you look beautiful in whatever you wear!'

'I know what you're saying, Didi. No need to stress. Um…are you *sure* Pierre will be coming at seven…um…it's just that it's *six now* and if he's not back yet…from wherever…'

'Oh, course he'll be back in time! I think he may just have popped down to the local for a beer. You know what men are like! Doesn't matter how devoted they are, they still need a bit of down time now and again! Charlie, as you well know, was fond of telling me that his Fridays were sacrosanct. Said he needed his weekly injection of male sanity.'

Georgie had other ideas about the nature of the sanity Pierre might have needed. The faces of several of the pretty young teachers sprang to mind.

And of course he was free, single and unencumbered! He could do as he wanted. She sourly gave voice to her jealousy. She called it disappointment.

She raided her limited wardrobe and decided that she was now free from the constraints of having to dress for him, either because she needed to be seen to make an effort by Didi, or because she just wanted to prove to him that she didn't care what he thought of her. She would dress for herself…and for the clientele of smart diners who would be at the restaurant.

It was cold but she didn't intend to let the weather dictate her outfit.

A black and white woollen miniskirt, legacy of a long-forgotten university era, a tight black jumper with a flattering cowl neck, which was the last word in impracticality considering her neck would freeze, and some high black boots even though she was sorely tempted to dress down by wearing her usual flats.

And her hair. Out came the straighteners and, at the end of half an hour, the curly fly-away hair and bane of her life had been tamed into submission and lay in a flat, shiny sheet down her back. Not bad. In fact, rather startling, Georgie thought, doing a little twirl. It wasn't very often that all three aspects of her appearance came together. Normally the outfit would be let down by the shoes, or the shoes by the hair…the list was endless, but tonight…

She carried on marvelling at her reflection when the doorbell went at seven and then she took her time teetering on her high heels to answer the door.

'Oh, hullo,' she said frostily. He was wearing a bow-tie but it was undone and his black coat was slung carelessly over him. He looked as if he had exited the house in a hurry and probably had, she thought sourly. Drinks down at the local *would* put a person behind schedule. 'I'll just fetch my coat.'

Pierre leaned against the door and watched her. He should have left the school and headed straight back, but no. Instead he had veered off in the opposite direction and, like a loser, had sat on his own in the pub nursing a pint, which had done nothing for his frame of mind. He felt irritable and trapped by a peculiar sense of indecision. He was almost surprised when she returned, shrugging on her coat and then glancing around her the way people did when checking their house one last time before leaving it. For a few seconds he had been miles away. And not thinking about work. Thinking about…he rubbed his eyes and stepped outside. He wasn't quite sure what he *had* been thinking about. He only knew that he would have to get his life back in order and soon.

CHAPTER EIGHT

'THANK you for what you did this afternoon.' This to break the silence stretching between them. All semblance of pleasantries, Georgie noticed, seemed to have bitten the dust. Not one comment on her appearance, never mind that Pierre had always felt free to be derogatory about it in the past. Even that would have been preferable to his stony silence, which she could only put down to his disappointment at having to drag himself away from the charms of her fellow colleagues and wherever they had gone after she had left.

'I told you that I would. I expect you assumed that I would let you down.'

'No! Of course not!' More awkward silence. 'You made a very good Santa Claus,' she continued, clearing her throat. 'Very convincing, all things considered. The kids loved you. Really good idea to get them sitting around you like that.'

'Good.'

'Didi says we're going to that new fish restaurant.'

'Yes.'

'That's a relief.' Course, she could give a hoot what he thought of her. 'Because I wouldn't want to end up anywhere overdressed.'

Pierre glanced briefly at her. She looked stunning. It was a description he had never imagined he would ever have used for her, but she did. 'You won't be,' he said shortly, returning his attention to the road.

'I'm sorry if you feel that you've had to drag yourself out to dinner with me,' Georgie burst out, increasingly irritated by his foul temper, for which she wasn't to blame. 'You could have made an excuse with Didi. I would have been more than happy to have cancelled.'

'I'm sure, but Didi would have been disappointed and I'm not having that. Whether you would have preferred to have ducked out is irrelevant.'

'In that case, the least you could do is to be polite.'

'I'm sorry. Is that not what I'm being?' He eased his car in front of the restaurant and killed the engine, but before getting out he swivelled around so that he was facing her, one arm resting loosely on the steering wheel.

In the shadowy darkness, his face was given harsh definition and Georgie had to remind herself that this was, after all, *just an ordinary human being*.

That consoling thought gave her the strength not to cringe back into the passenger door.

'Maybe you're piqued because I didn't compliment you on your feminine look,' he gritted. 'I don't flatter myself that the effort was for me, which isn't to say that I shouldn't have known that you would want to be noticed. So, is that it? Shall I help you along with your fishing session by telling you that you're a triumph of beauty?' Pierre felt as though he had reverted to being a teenager again and worse, a teenager who hadn't got his way with the girl he was after. He raked his fingers through his hair and looked away, angry with himself for his loss of self-control.

'I wasn't *fishing*,' Georgie told him, reddening. She swung to open the door and he let her, rousing himself after a few seconds and following her.

'I don't *care* what you think of me!' Georgie informed him as he pushed open the door and allowed her to sweep past him. In her wake, she left that clean, vaguely floral scent that he realised he now associated with her. The woman had bewitched him, with her ridiculous outfits and yapping personality and with supermarket perfume that filled his nostrils and left him wanting more.

Pierre didn't know who he cared for less in this unwelcome scenario. Himself for being weak or her for just being *her.*

If he had slept with her, he knew that this would not now be posing a problem. He was a predator who enjoyed the chase as much as the capture. The fact that Georgie had eluded him had succeeded in doing the one thing no woman had done before—it had buried the thought of her deep inside him, taking away his ability to think clearly, making him a victim of his own basic desires.

From behind, as they were shown to their table his eyes lingered on the boyish swing of her hips and the slimness of her legs, for once not concealed underneath flowing, hippy layers. Her hair hung down her back and he wanted to reach out and grab it and pull her back into him, he wanted to crush her mouth with his and taste her surrender. In short, he wanted everything he had been denied.

The restaurant was buzzing, despite the bracing temperatures outside. He wondered how he could ever have summed the place up as a backwater with only limited accessibility to mod cons.

'Shall we try again?' he asked as soon as they were seated. 'We're here. We might as well behave as adults and enjoy the evening.'

Georgie looked at him warily. 'You're the one who seems keen to pick a fight with me.'

Pierre, in that instant, was faced with the unthinkable re-alisation that he would release his much-cherished pride and pursue this woman despite the knock-back. It was either that or be driven crazy from frustration.

He looked down and then straight at her. 'You could be right,' he agreed, and he was gratified to see her eyes widen in surprise. 'I'll be man enough to admit that you've got under my skin.' He made no move to lean towards her or even to invest his words with any sense of urgency. Instead, he shrugged. 'I can't stop thinking of you.' He let that indis-putable truth drop like a stone into a pond and waited for the ripples to spread out. 'In fact, you very nearly made me lose concentration at my meeting yesterday. Not good. A success-ful businessman doesn't start talking about management buyouts only to end up staring out of the window because he's completely lost his train of thought.' Pierre spotted the waitress out of the corner of his eye and beckoned her over, although he remained looking at Georgie, even when he ordered them a bottle of white wine.

'I…I don't believe you…'

'Why would I lie?' The wine had arrived. He tasted it, watching her over the rim of his glass, and then nodded for the waitress to pour. 'You haunt me,' he told her casually. 'I can even recognise your smell.'

'D-don't be silly,' Georgie stammered, feeling suddenly exposed in her daring little outfit behind which she couldn't con-veniently hide. She quickly gulped down some wine, then a little more, until she realised that the glass was empty. Not for long.

'And I *did* notice your outfit tonight, by the way…'

'Did you?' she squeaked.

'How could I not? I bet that's your one and only miniskirt.'

'It's…I…'

He had thrown her into a state of confusion, which seemed

only right considering that was the place she had so neatly managed to stick him. 'Never mind that most girls your age have wardrobes of them. Still…you don't have a problem looking utterly desirable in whatever you wear. How did you manage to get your hair to look like that?'

'Straighteners,' Georgie answered, flustered.

'I prefer it curly, though. Curly hair suits your personality. But enough of all this. I don't suppose you want to hear how I feel about you. Nothing worse than someone who continues the chase when the game is over…' Pierre swirled his glass and stared at her, allowing his words to sink in. He might not be the sort of man much interested in laying his feelings on the line, but, with the instincts of someone highly attuned to female behaviour, he ruthlessly exploited that most dangerous of all emotions—curiosity. And she *was* curious, even though he could see her warring feelings written on her face. He had taken her by surprise and, having opened an unexpected door behind which he had invited her to peep, he was now about to shut it, leaving her wanting more.

She opened her mouth to say something, but he expertly changed the topic and began chatting to her harmlessly about his drive down from London.

Who cared about his drive down from London? Georgie thought. It was *wrong* but what she really wanted to hear was more about his feelings for her. She *knew*, in her head, that it all amounted to the same thing—passing lust—but how different it sounded when he was looking at her with those stunning eyes, not demanding a thing, just telling her what he thought. She surfaced to find that he was asking her something and immediately answered to discover that she had said yes to another bottle of wine. Where on earth had number one gone?

'We really shouldn't drink much more,' she felt obliged to tell him. 'I mean, you're driving. How are we going to get back?'

'I have only been sipping my wine. Georgia. Tell me about the people you work with. They seem a nice bunch.'

Georgie was beginning to feel pleasantly light-headed, a combination of the wine and the headiness of his words. Mention of her colleagues brought her back down to earth with a bump.

'They're very nice,' she agreed, thinking of Claudette, Janice and Liz, last spotted batting their eyelashes and flirting as though sightings of attractive men were a rare event to be enjoyed before they vanished.

'Now why do I get the feeling that you're not being entirely sincere?' Pierre frowned. 'Is there some sort of problem there, Georgie? Small places can get a bit hothouse, especially when the crew are largely female and roughly the same age.' It wasn't like Georgie to be reticent in her friendliness. He felt a sudden and powerful urge to protect her even though he knew very well that she could be as ferocious as a bulldog when it suited her. 'Is there some kind of bullying going on? I don't suppose there would be anyone to complain to…'

'What on earth are you talking about, Pierre?' Georgie asked, astonished at his train of thought, which had sprung from nowhere and seemed to be heading for destinations unknown.

'I'm talking about what's going on in that school of yours. You're obviously not happy there.'

'I'm very happy there.'

'Then why the tone of voice when I mentioned the girls you worked with?' Her change of expression said it all and Pierre gave her a slow, knowing smile. 'Ah. I see.'

'See what?'

'No need to be jealous.'

'Jealous? Me?'

'Jealous. You. Now then, what are you going to have? To eat?' Georgie hadn't even noticed the arrival of the waitress.

She glanced down at her menu, flustered by the way he kept leading her along only to leave her high and dry by changing the subject. How had he known that she was jealous? She had barely admitted to the emotion herself! She ordered the freshly caught fish of the day from the menu and wondered whether he would now start talking about something utterly boring and harmless, maybe the weather or her work. They had already killed the tedious subject of motorway traffic.

'Good choice.' Pierre snapped shut his menu and poured her another glass of wine. 'Not everyone would have had the gumption to order the dressed crab. Now where were we? Oh, yes. You were going to tell me why you're jealous of your colleagues. I only chatted to them, although…' He pretended to ponder an interesting possibility that was taking place in his head.

'Although what?'

'You're pouting.'

'I'm not *pouting*. I don't *pout*, Pierre. Anyway, I'm drinking far too much. I need to get some food inside me.'

'You should have had something a little more substantial for starters than the smoked salmon salad,' he mused. He signalled for some bread, which Georgie dived into in an attempt to steady her frayed nerves.

'You were saying…' she reminded him. 'Actually not so much saying as *thinking about* one of my colleagues.' She gave a light laugh that tried and failed to sound carefree. 'Typical of you to tell me that you find *me* attractive only to spoil the effect by lusting after Janice.'

'What makes you think that it was Janice?'

'Long brown hair? Big blue eyes? Cleavage in full display even in winter?' How catty did she sound? 'That was horrible. I take it back.'

'I prefer green eyes anyway…'

Georgie could feel dangerous recklessness steal into her

well-erected defences and begin to chip away at them. She would have been able to cope with a full-fledged assault, but these sexy, lazy compliments and the way his eyes were drinking her in made her feel hot and bothered and warmly, wetly excited.

She looked away, concentrating on what she was eating, but her hands were trembling. She heard herself make some stupid remark about how tasty the food was. The truth was that she was barely aware of what she was eating.

Regret, like a thief, crept into her heart, plundering her moralistic views about sex and love being entwined.

She wasn't sure whether to be relieved or disappointed when he quickly took up the mantle of polite chit-chat that she threw to him and began telling her about some of the weird things he had eaten in the course of his travels.

But the way he looked at her... Georgie wondered whether it might be the wine turning her brain to cotton wool, whether she was imagining the brush of his fingers against hers as he helped her with the dressed crab, which she had to apparently dissect with some peculiar instruments. He adroitly fished some of the meat from a claw and offered it to her on a small fork and the gesture seemed almost *seductive*.

'I feel a little giddy,' Georgie said abruptly, pushing her plate to one side and taking a few deep breaths. She closed her eyes for a couple of seconds and opened them to find him staring at her in concern.

'Describe.'

'Light-headed? Woozy? Grateful that I'm sitting down because I might fall over if I stand up? That sort of giddy?' To prove her point, she stood up only to sink back into her chair. 'You gave me too much wine!' she accused balefully.

'Oh, no, you don't,' Pierre said, but in a soft, mildly reproving voice, as if gently chastising a wilful child. 'I didn't hold a gun to your head and force you to drink. You wanted to drink because…' He paused and waited for her to ask him to expand on his statement.

'Because you didn't want to come here tonight…'

'I suppose…' Georgie thought, confusedly, that she might not have wanted to come, but she had certainly enjoyed the evening. Enjoyed it in the way someone enjoyed a roller-coaster ride—with fear, trepidation and excitement. All unexpected.

'I'll get the bill. We'll leave.'

She leaned into him as they left the restaurant and, once outside, the cold air restored some of her diminished equilibrium. At least the giddy feeling was beginning to recede.

'Thanks for the evening.' She turned to him as soon as he had pulled up outside her house, which looked coldly, darkly uninviting. She should have left the light in the downstairs sitting room on.

'Not so fast.' Pierre opened his car door and stepped out, not giving her the chance to argue. 'I'm not leaving you in this state,' he murmured and as she fumbled out of the passenger side he lifted her off her feet and walked towards the front door. One impractical shoe, dangling from her foot, fell and was ignored.

'Put me down,' Georgie protested weakly.

'Sure. As soon as we're inside. Give me your key.'

Georgie yawned and extracted the key from her bag. Not just the one key, but an array of them all pegged together on a key chain that seemed to contain everything but the kitchen sink. Pierre was pretty sure that it jangled loudly enough to rouse every resident on the street. Totally impractical, needless to say. But incredibly sweet.

He kicked open the door and then nudged it shut behind him, fumbling to find the light switch but not ready to put her down.

'Coffee,' he told her, when he finally rested her gently on

the sofa in the sitting room. 'Black and sweet. And water. At least a bottle.'

'Yuk.'

'Don't fall asleep on me,' he warned, leaving the room. 'If you don't rehydrate, you'll wake up with the most God Almighty hangover.'

He returned minutes later and carefully sat her up so that he could make her take tiny sips of water.

'I don't need you to do that, Pierre.' Georgie hiccupped. 'I'm not *that* far gone.'

'I want to,' he murmured softly, which sent a thrilling little tingle racing down her spine. He positioned her so that he was sitting behind her and she was lying against him, with her back to his chest and her soft, silky hair threading across his face.

If she couldn't feel his erection, then she really must be in the land of sweet dreams because he could feel it pushing against his trouser zip, big and hard and pulsing. He shifted his body weight and she sighed against him, a soft, purring sound that made him clench his jaw in frustration.

'Feeling better?' he wrenched out and she nodded and sighed again, then, agonisingly for him, she wriggled against him and then she stilled.

'I should go,' he murmured. 'You can feel the effect you're having on me.'

Georgie discovered that the last thing she wanted was for him to go. She squirmed until she was facing him, her legs straddling his hips, then she lightly sat on him, feeling his hardness rub against her tights and underwear, powerful and rigid even through the layers of cloth separating them.

Since this was precisely what he had wanted, he could barely believe himself as he pushed her very gently off him and stood up.

Georgie looked up at him in disbelief.

'Don't look at me like that.' He raked his fingers through his hair and half sighed, half groaned. 'Don't think it's not what I want. It is. I've told you how I feel about you. Twice now by my reckoning.'

'Don't go. I don't want you to go.'

'You've had too much to drink. Call me old-fashioned—' he gave a crooked smile '—but I've never taken advantage of a woman under the influence of drink.'

'I won't tell if you don't.' She pulled the jumper over her head, revelling in the way he went completely still, as if he had drawn in his breath and could not now release it.

It felt good not to have the wool rubbing against her skin.

In one swift, easy movement, she removed her bra and then she lay back on the sofa and looked at him drowsily. She could see his bulging arousal and, taking her cue from that, she lifted her hands to her breasts and trailed her fingers across her nipples. They tightened into stiff buds and she moaned softly.

Pierre looked at her, mesmerised. Her body was smooth and pale and as she breathed her breasts rose and fell, small and pert and her perfect, pink nipples... He briefly closed his eyes to block out the tantalising image.

'I like you looking at me,' Georgie said, and Pierre wondered whether she would be saying that were she stone-cold sober. More likely she would have coldly thanked him for a *nice* evening and then shut the door quietly but firmly in his face. She reached to pull down her skirt but before she could take that step further he was in front of her, lifting her from the sofa and, regardless of her alcohol intake, he slung her over his shoulder and headed for the stairs while she fruitlessly pummelled his back with her fists and demanded to be put down *immediately*.

'No chance,' Pierre muttered savagely under his breath. 'You're going to bed right now for both our sakes.'

It didn't help him that he was very much aware of her breasts squashing against his shoulder blades.

Her room was in complete darkness. Didn't the woman leave *any* lights on when she left the house at night? Or did she think it was fun to fumble blindly for switches?

While he fumbled, she continued to complain but she fell silent as he laid her on her bed and stood back to look at her cautiously.

'I'll bring you up some water.'

'Okay.'

'Good. Okay.' He hovered, frowning. 'Stay right there,' he added pointlessly and she nodded.

Literally he ran and then returned to the bedroom, taking the stairs two at a time. She was already beginning to drift off. He left the glass by the bedside table and then went across to the window and drew the curtains.

And that was how Georgie awoke, disoriented, wrenched out of sleep by the weirdest of dreams and now up, incredibly thirsty.

As her eyes adjusted she blinked, trying to get her bearings, and gave a little startled yelp at the shadowy bulk in the chair by the window.

Without thinking, she switched on the bedside light, and at the same time Pierre stirred and in the thick silence their eyes tangled. Belatedly, Georgie realised that she was undressed. No top, no skirt, no tights. The memory of the night before came in a rush, the wine, her impromptu striptease on the sofa, being carried upstairs, caveman-style. The only gap in her memory was how she ended up completely undressed and she assumed he had done that, eased her skirt off along with her tights. And instead of going, he had stayed, was here now.

She wrapped her arms over her exposed breasts.

'I'll go.' Pierre stood up. 'How do you feel?'

'I feel…' she frowned and looked up at him, towering in darkness at the side of her bed '…very sober now. A little thirsty, but that's all.' She took the water from the side table and drank a long mouthful. 'And I feel that I still don't want you to go, Pierre.'

'What's changed?' he heard himself asking. Having wilfully created a window of opportunity, he now, perversely, felt uncomfortable with the outcome, even though it was in his favour. He couldn't work it out. Was it because she was just so much more vulnerable than the women he had dated in the past? 'The last time we spoke you told me in no uncertain terms that sex was all about the fairy-tale ending.'

'Dreams of fairy-tale endings don't make good bed companions…' And she loved him. Loved him and wanted him and needed him and would take whatever he offered because it would always be better than nothing.

'No,' Pierre agreed, 'they don't.' He began taking off his shirt and Georgie felt her heartbeat quicken.

'Why did you stay?' she asked, embarrassed at the way in which she was shamelessly devouring him with her eyes.

'I wanted to make sure you were going to be okay,' Pierre said truthfully.

'I'm useless with alcohol.' She lay back against the pillows and let her arms fall to her sides, at once shy of her body and yet turned on by her own daring.

'Nice.' He paused in his tracks and feasted on the sight of her. His shirt was off. Now he pulled the belt from his trousers in one easy movement and unzipped them. He had the perfect, well-honed body of a man who worked out. Well, he did, didn't he? And probably pushed himself as ferociously in the gym as he did in every other aspect of his life. His shoulders were broad and she could see the definition of his stomach muscles. The man wasn't just *good-looking*. How could she ever have thought that? The man took sexiness to new extremes. She felt like a maiden in a Victorian melodrama on the verge of swooning.

'Do you like what you see?' Pierre asked, amused by her blatant absorption with his body. He walked closer to the bed. Only the sheer strength of his will-power prevented him from rushing, from taking her quickly so that his body could be satisfied. 'Pull down those covers. I want to see all of you. Nothing on.'

She obeyed so that she was lying in full view and, instead of reacting with feminist outrage that she was being looked at solely as a sexual object, she felt herself melting, wanting this man to just do what he wanted to do.

When, naked, he did finally join her in bed, it was as if she were coming home, returning to a place she knew and from which she should never be made to leave.

Fierce thrills washed over her as he supported himself over her, bending so that he could ravage her mouth with his, his tongue probing relentlessly, and she revelled in the feel of him as she scraped her fingers along his back and parted her legs so that she could feel the steady rub of him against her.

'Glad I stayed?' he growled, wanting to hear her *say it* and she did, eyes closed, her body panting to his rhythm.

Satisfied, he began exploring her body, inch by responsive inch, starting with her breasts, licking and nipping them with such lazy expertise that she arched up and cried out, soft moans that were wrenched out of her, sending his already hungry body into yet more agonising overdrive.

While he sucked her breasts, his fingers sought out her wet, swollen bud sheathed in damp, fair curls and he began teasing it.

'When was the last time you made love?' he asked.

'Can't remember. Ages ago.'

'Maybe you were subconsciously waiting for me. Am I worth the wait?'

'Every minute…'

Those were the two most erotic words he had ever heard and he groaned thickly, reaching for her hand so that he could show her how he liked to be touched.

His lack of inhibitions in bed were a revelation to her. He knew what she wanted and how she wanted it and he was overcome with an urge to make sure his every touch was exquisite, memorable. He trailed hot kisses along her quivering stomach, nuzzled the soft flesh of her breasts, then clasped his hands under her bottom so that he could bring her to his mouth.

This was beyond anything Georgie could ever have imagined, having this glorious, powerful man shudder as he tasted her and explored her with his darting tongue, knowing that just the feel and the touch of her could ignite such fierce abandon.

When they reversed positions so that they could mutually taste each other, she could feel the same desperate passion contained in his body as was in hers and it gave her a confidence she had never thought possible. How could she doubt her own attractiveness to him when it was *tangible*?

And thinking for her, he was aware enough to enquire about protection.

'I'll be fine.' She didn't want him to stop and she wanted more than just oral stimulation. She wanted so much to feel him inside her, filling her up.

Pierre heaved himself up alongside her and cupped her breast in his hand, bringing her down from the heights to which he had taken her. 'You'll be fine? What does that mean, my darling?'

Georgie wondered whether she had heard correctly. Had he just called her *my darling?* It was a meaningless term of endearment, of course, but still…

'Please don't stop,' she begged.

Pierre lowered his head and gently suckled on her nipple. This was dangerous territory. No contraception and, worse, he was tempted to trust in fate. It wasn't going to do. Fate had a nasty habit of backfiring and what would he do if a moment's passion resulted in a pregnancy?

He had a fleeting vision of a tiny blonde-haired green-eyed toddler and swept the thought aside as quickly as it had arrived.

Sex was one thing. Reality was something entirely different.

'There are other ways of being satisfied,' he murmured, 'and it will make the next time all the better for having waited.'

His hand strayed down and he touched her again, proving his point.

Their love-making was slow and languorous and took them into the early hours of the morning. Somewhere along the line, lying in the dark, they talked about Didi and, in between, about their own childhood experiences.

Okay. He admitted that it wasn't the kind of conversation he usually had in bed with a woman, but he had virtually grown up with this one, in a manner of speaking. Anyway, they were bound to discuss Didi at some point considering she was virtually the reason they had ended up in bed together, and the progression from Didi to other related family matters was hardly surprising, especially when they were in bed, her head resting in the crook of his arm and his hand lightly playing with her soft nipple.

Of the future nothing was said. The sexual relationship that she had adamantly refused to have was now a given. When, sleepily, she asked him what Didi would think if she woke up to find him absent, he simply shrugged and rolled on his side to face her.

'She's probably been surprised that I haven't stayed the night here before,' he told her dryly. 'She'll be thrilled.'

'Not too thrilled, I hope,' Georgie said, tentatively treading on thin ice. 'We wouldn't want her believing that wedding bells are just around the corner, would we?'

'Lord, no.' Pierre could feel, again, the uneasy step of fate waiting round the corner with a bagful of nasty surprises. Not worth thinking about. 'But, sweetheart…' he pushed his thigh between hers and began moving it slowly until she was squirming against him and giving soft little grunts of pleasure '…this is for real. No more pretending to convince my mother that we're an item. When I touch you in front of her…' he paused and Georgie wriggled on his thigh, loving the friction of his muscle against her wet, aroused femininity '…it will be for real. Everything will be so much easier.'

Georgie heard the rider in the statement and closed her eyes on a sigh.

So much easier not to pretend, so much easier to tell the truth when the break-up happens. All round the perfect solution and incredible sex in the bargain.

She couldn't think of any of that, not just now when she could feel her body building up to the steady rhythm, like a wave rising to its peak.

Besides, she was an optimist and who knew what tomorrow would bring?

CHAPTER NINE

IT BROUGHT more than Georgie had ever expected. Instead of the run-up to Christmas being the usual routine of shopping for presents for close friends, putting up her Christmas tree on her own with her Christmas carol CD blaring in the background and after-work parties where wine played a very big part, this time Pierre was around.

Georgie didn't like to ask him about work, just in case he remembered where he had mislaid it. The fact was she could never have imagined that he was capable of being as relaxed as he was. If he was, indeed, beavering away behind the scenes on his computer, then he was being extremely efficient at hiding the fact because they were together most days and only twice had she seen him take calls on his mobile. Unavoidable, he had apologised.

This, Georgie assumed, was the carefree period Pierre had mentioned, the one during which they could enjoy each other before, for him at least, those twin curses of familiarity and contempt set in and he became restless, eager to move on to other pastures.

Although the weather was not conducive to seeing the countryside at its best, they still did a lot of touristy stuff. Georgie was appalled at how unfamiliar he was with the surroundings in which he had spent his childhood, until he reminded her that the better part of his childhood was spent in the confines of a boarding school.

'Which suited me perfectly,' he was at pains to assure her. 'An only child is a lonely child. I was surrounded by kids my own age. It couldn't have been better, especially considering Charlie and Didi spent most of their waking hours trying to make a go of the farm.'

'Did you resent them for that?' Georgie asked, but he gave her one of his eloquent shrugs, a signal for her to steer clear of quizzing him. Those shrugs had become fewer and farther between. She didn't know whether he had noticed that but *she* had. She was making inroads into his private thoughts and she delighted in that. He was a revelation to her and there was nothing about him that she didn't want to explore.

Of course, when Christmas was done and dusted, reality would set in. He would return to London and once he was back in the swing of life there, with its high-voltage, frenetic pace, he would soon forget his lazy times in Devon, but until then Georgie was happy to bask in the pleasure of doing things with him. His knowledge of even minor things was vast and, like a squirrel, she stored away the memory of evenings spent at Didi's cottage, in front of the open fire in the sitting room, listening to him tell them about his travels and teasing him that he couldn't really call them *travels* when they involved him being inside an office working, even if the office was on the other side of the world.

And of course she bought him a present. It had taken ages to choose because she had to toe the fine line between personal and impersonal.

Pierre might enjoy being with her but theirs was a tacit understanding that nothing was for ever, least of all their re-lationship. He didn't do clingy. The merest hint that she was taking what they had more seriously than he was would guarantee his immediate flight. She had come to the conclusion that he was a man who kept a supply of running shoes very close to hand should he need them to escape a woman who might be getting too close for comfort.

So her present was a book. He had mentioned, in one of those moments of unconscious intimacy, that his favourite book when he had first gone to boarding school and was still settling in was *The Adventures of Huckleberry Finn*. She had had an image of lonely little boy hunkered down under the covers with a torch, reading about someone else's adventures to take his mind off the isolation of being somewhere strange for the first time. Naturally she had avoided sharing that insight with him. It would definitely have warranted one of those shrugs. But she had managed to find an early copy of the book on eBay, complete with hand painted illustrations. Surely that couldn't be mistaken for being too personal?

On Christmas Eve, after a week and a glorious half of suspended reality, the three of them went to early service at the church and then back to Didi's for supper. It had taken very little to persuade Georgie to stay the night so that they could all wake up bright and early on Christmas morning for present unwrapping, and she had duly been transported by Pierre with clothes, gifts and various bits and pieces of food.

'I feel as though I'm moving house,' she joked, stepping out of the Bentley and looking at him with laughter in her eyes.

'Oh, I can't see you leaving your chickens that readily,' Pierre answered, and she felt a shadow flicker across the brightness of her mood but she banished it with another laugh.

'Don't you think they would be able to fend for themselves?'

'Not the way you've mollycoddled them. What on earth have you packed in this case, Georgie? It weighs a ton.'

A note of defensiveness crept into her voice. 'I've brought my presents. Stuffed them in alongside some clothes.'

'I suppose it's a woman's right to travel heavy,' Pierre said, unlocking the front door and pushing it open with his foot so that he could heave her case into the hall. Didi was asleep. Having wanted to stay up so that the three of them could enjoy a glass of port around the tree before turning in, she had found the day too long for her in the end and they had settled her up to bed before heading off to Georgie's house to collect her things. 'But you're only staying over for one night! How many change of outfits can one person need for one night and a day?'

'I brought a bit extra just in case I ended up staying longer than planned,' Georgie confessed. 'I've been caught out twice now having to spend the night somewhere without a change of clothes. I decided to take a few precautions this time.' This was one of those moments when she was reminded of the impermanence of their situation and she wasn't about to face it head-on. Not on Christmas Eve.

She skipped towards the staircase and looked back at him over her shoulder with a pretence of sultriness, eyelashes fluttering, smile coy. She had teased him some time ago that since he was probably a dab hand at dealing with women who did things like flutter their lashes, and since she had never done that before, then she would practise on him, but then she had taken it back, saying that she had forgotten that his women were too busy thinking about the World Economy to have time for lash-fluttering. He had laughed but hadn't denied it and now, ever so often, she would play the sex siren just for the heck of it.

She preceded him into his bedroom while he lugged her suitcase in and complained of sudden backache.

'Shall I massage it for you?' Georgie asked innocently.

Pierre straightened and grinned at her. 'I am constantly amazed,' he murmured softly, 'at what a wanton little thing you have turned out to be.' He stripped off the worn rugby jumper he had stuck on earlier and began undoing the buttons of his shirt. 'You've even put away the hippy clothes…'

'Only because I'm not going to school at the moment,' Georgie said loftily, just in case he got it into his head that he had managed to alter her dress sense along with everything else. 'There's no need to dress quite so sensibly. Anyway, we've been to a Church service! Of course I'm going to look smart!'

Pierre held up his hands in mock surrender but his eyes were laughing. 'Okay, okay!' He stripped off the shirt and then proceeded to divest himself of the remainder of his clothes.

She still hadn't quite become accustomed to the grace and beauty of his body. Every time he stood in front of her, naked and at no pains to conceal his erection, she was reduced to blushing self-consciousness.

'I'm ready for my massage.' He stepped towards her and began describing in graphic detail what he wanted her to do to him, then he lay down on the bed, his hand resting lightly on his proud member, and commanded her to undress. Very slowly. And as she undressed he told her what she should do, which part of her body she should touch.

'Lessons from a master,' she murmured, smiling and slinking her way towards him on the bed.

'And you'll thank me for that one fine day.' Pierre had a strong urge to remind her of that. This break from routine was extraordinarily refreshing, as was her hot little body in bed with his every night and during the day as well, in some very imaginative places. But it would come to an end. He knew that because he knew that his real life was waiting for him in a week's time. The new year would see him returned to the heady business of running his empire.

'What do you mean?' Georgie asked, drawing in her breath ever so slightly so that she could feel her chest beginning to ache.

She couldn't meet his eyes and thankfully he turned over onto his stomach, flexing the muscles in his broad back.

'I mean think of the ways you would have learnt in bed to impress your man.' He had been far more impressed teaching *her* than he could ever have been by any woman being skilled and acrobatic between the sheets, but somehow it felt dangerous to allow that thought to sneak in, let alone voice it.

Georgie forced herself to smile as she began working her magic on his back, enjoying the feel of his firm flesh under her fingers.

'How right you are,' she said lightly.

Immediately Pierre wondered whether she had someone in mind. As far as he knew there were no men on the scene and hadn't been for a while, but was there someone lurking in the periphery of her vision? Another up-and-coming journalist, perhaps, waiting to bowl her over with a bit of surface banter and intellectual intensity that she was probably impressed by?

Never one to harbour any self-doubt, Pierre had a sudden and uncomfortable suspicion that he was just a blip on her horizon. Which, he told himself, was just as well, considering she was just that on his, but still…

He rolled over onto his back and, where she would have lain next to him, he manoeuvred her onto his stomach so that she was straddling him, every bit of her exposed for him. He liked that. He idly played with his hand between her thighs enjoying how he made her feel. Wet and aroused and breathless.

But he wanted to talk to her, not have her move against his hand, with her head thrown back and her eyes closed. Her small breasts bounced as she moved heatedly and he raised his free hand to toy with her nipple, watching as she shuddered in immediate response.

Unable to help himself, he edged her up to him so that he could smell the sweet fragrance of her, so that his tongue was within flicking distance of that sensitised bud that, even lightly touched, could have her groaning and begging for more.

Talk would come in a minute. For now, he couldn't resist the inviting essence of her and he brought her to his mouth, clasping his hands behind her buttocks so that he could knead them as he tasted every drop of the sweet juice between her legs.

When she would have eased down to further their love-making, however, he gently rolled her to her side so that she was facing him and looked at her seriously,

'What is it?' Georgie eyed him anxiously. 'You look as though you're about to say *There's something I need to tell you…*' She laughed a little nervously because sentences that started in that way didn't usually herald good tidings. What would she do if he decided that it was all over between them? A sudden void opened up in front of her, a yawning chasm that was terrifying in its emptiness.

'We need to talk,' he said, as kindly as he could although he was already seething inside at imaginary scenarios in which she brought her specials talents in bed to someone else to sample, some long-haired, bearded vegetarian who would probably charm his way into her life by feigning interest in her chickens. And she, newly released from a life of sexual in-activity, would of course be as horny as hell and rearing to go.

'What about?'

'About you, actually.' Pierre thought about how to phrase his next statement without sounding patronising and then decided that he didn't care *how* he sounded. 'I don't know how to say this, Georgie…'

'*You* don't know how to say something, Pierre?' Georgie laughed, but her heart was beating furiously with a mixture of dread and panic. 'That's a first. I must remember to write it in my diary tomorrow!'

'You're not experienced in…men—'

'Yes, but—'

'Let me finish. Being inexperienced makes you vulnerable and you're even more vulnerable than the average inexperienced woman because you're impulsive, you do things without thinking them through first.'

'I don't know where you're going with this,' she said, stung, but Pierre, having gathered the necessary momentum, ignored her protest.

'You'll walk into the arms of another man because you'll feel confident of your sexual abilities and you won't take time out to really check where you're going, work out who you're going to hand over your body and heart to…' He could hear himself losing the kindly tone of voice and took a deep, steadying breath. 'All I'm saying is that you have to be careful. There are a lot of sharks out there.'

Georgie, having expected a 'Dear John' speech, wasn't sure whether to feel relieved that she wasn't being ditched or irritated because he thought she was an idiot.

'I can take care of myself, Pierre.' She lay flat on her back, staring up at the ceiling.

'Can you? Can you?' He pulled her back to face him and, as expected, she was wearing a mutinous expression that made him all the more determined to make her see his point of view. 'You're a sexy, hot-blooded woman, Georgie, and I should know. You could have any man you wanted but are you going to make the right choices?'

'Probably not,' she admitted, thinking of the number-one wrong choice she had already made, which was to fall for *him,* the one man guaranteed to bring her heartbreak and misery.

'And *that's* supposed to reassure me?' he demanded roughly.

'What can I say? Life's full of chances. How do you know if you're going to end up involved with the wrong man?'

These weren't the answers Pierre wanted to hear, although he didn't really know *what* he wanted to hear. Perhaps that she would return to her state of cheerful singledom, but fat chance of that now that the joy of sex had reared its ugly head.

He resolved that in future he would make sure to avoid having other people's welfare at heart. Here he was, trying to give her some helpful advice, and in return she was pretty much confirming that she would launch forth into the heady world of men mentally programmed to make mistakes.

'Anyway…thanks very much for the advice, but don't we have better things to do in bed than talk about what might or might not happen at some point in the future?' The last thing she wanted was to think about that particular place. If she could hold back the hands of time then she would. 'I might, just might…' She conjured up in her head the ideal scenario: no more games; Pierre madly in love with her; in due course a white wedding, or at least a cream one, and thereafter the pitter patter of tiny feet '…find my ideal soul mate, the man I've been searching for all my life. These things have been known to happen, you know. It's not a given that I'll be unlucky enough to run slap bang into a man who's going to use me and then toss me aside.'

'And who would this ideal man be?' Pierre demanded.

You. But of course it would never do to say that, not if she wanted any kind of time with him. 'Oh, just someone kind and thoughtful and considerate with a good sense of humour.'

'A real high-flyer, in other words,' Pierre said tersely.

'You know I'm not very materialistic. Sometimes the happiest people are the ones who don't have much.'

'So you're in search of a down-and-out who can laugh at his situation while asking if he can borrow some money to buy you flowers and take you out for a romantic meal.'

'This is a silly conversation.' And the first argument they

had had in a while and Georgie didn't like it. She stroked his stomach, feeling his tension in the tautness of his muscles. Frankly, she had no idea why he was in a mood. Did he expect her to fall at his feet in gratitude because he had seen fit to try and tell her how to lead her life? Didn't he know how hurtful it was to realise that behind his words was the reality that their break-up was a given? *When she found someone else.* How much more direct could he get? All he hadn't done was to put a time limit on his eventual departure.

'I'll be fine,' she reassured him, just in case he had thought her response too flippant. She slid her hand along his thigh and he caught it in his, his dark expression indicating that he had more to say, but actually he just sighed and released her hand.

'You were saying something about better things to do in bed…' he queried roughly. 'Maybe you'd like to show me what exactly you had in mind.'

They woke to find an idyllic scene outside. The weathermen had forecasted snow and the heavens had obliged, opening up at some point during the early hours of the morning to deposit a blanket of white everywhere, and it was still snowing.

Pierre opened his eyes to see Georgie gazing in wonder out of the bedroom window and he slung his legs over the side and walked up behind her, wrapping his arms around her.

'Merry Christmas, my darling. Didn't I tell you what a good idea it was to travel with lots of spare clothing?' He kissed the nape of her neck and she smiled back at his reflection.

'Isn't it gorgeous?'

'I don't like it when you stick a nightie on. I prefer to have your hot body naked next to mine.'

'Awkward when it comes to going to the bathroom in the middle of the night,' Georgie pointed out. 'This house gets cold in winter when the heater goes off.'

'Mmm. But when you're clothed it's more difficult for me to do this...' Their eyes met in the window and she watched his strong, elegant hands push up the oversized tee shirt that she used as nightwear so that they could cup her breasts and massage them, his thumbs rolling over her nipples until she was panting softly and leaning back against him, her eyelids fluttering.

'Someone could see us,' she whispered unsteadily and he grinned.

'How many people are going to be strolling through open fields in the snow on Christmas morning? Oh, look! There's a queue of them!'

Georgie straightened automatically, but of course he was joking.

He wasn't, however, joking about what he wanted to do. He removed the tee shirt and, Georgie having left off her underwear, they were both now naked in front of the window, which offered them a tantalising reflection of themselves, with Pierre leaning over her, one hand moving over her breasts while the other drifted lower.

'We have to go downstairs...' Georgie gasped and laughed at the same time. 'Didi's probably already fussing in the kitchen waiting for us to appear! It's gone eight!'

'Which is why we're not going to be very long,' he murmured in response, 'much as I would like to be...' He spun her round and in one swift movement hoisted her up and onto him. She felt his hard shaft in her and her whole body juddered in response, then she began moving on him, deep and fast, secure in his embrace.

They came with explosive intensity, Pierre's big body jerking and stiffening, his head flung back, eyes closed.

It was a moment Georgie wished she could cling to for ever, especially considering their last conversation, which she had uneasily pushed to one side but hadn't quite managed to banish to complete oblivion.

As they dressed to go downstairs she could feel the little bubble she had built around them begin to wobble and then, her optimism rising once again to the surface, she thought, *Why be scared?*

She paused and looked at herself in the mirror. What she saw was a woman in love. Her cheeks were flushed, her eyes were bright, every bit of her was *alive*. Wrong man, admittedly. At least as far as security went, but, heck, why should she roll over and play dead? Really why should she *just assume* the inevitable?

Why, in other words, shouldn't she *fight for him?* It would have to be an underhand fight because he still had no idea how she truly felt about him, but she could do it!

He had already vanished downstairs. The bedroom door was open and she could hear the indistinct sounds of him talking to Didi. She knew one person who would heartily approve of her perseverance, should she have had an inkling of the true situation, and that was Didi. Didi, faced with a similar situation, would never have contemplated just hanging on and then giving up when the time came.

The solution...Georgie dabbed a little blush on her cheeks...was simple...she added just a hint of lip gloss so that her mouth looked even plumper and more inviting...she would make herself indispensable. She had until the new year, but in that period she would do her damnedest to ingratiate herself and then when he returned to London...who knew? Hadn't he already told her that he had missed her once before? He could miss her again and this time as his lover.

All dark thoughts dealt with, Georgie went downstairs to find a pot of freshly brewed coffee and hot croissants waiting on the kitchen table.

Didi was fussing around the turkey, which she had insisted was a traditional Christmas dish and on no accounts to be replaced by any upstart, such as fish, which had been Pierre and Georgie's suggestion. That one turkey, however modestly sized, would be far too big for three people, had met with a tart, 'I'm a dab hand at dealing with leftovers.'

Pierre gave her one of those secret half-smiles that made her toes curl and when she sat down he dropped a kiss lightly on the top of her head.

Then, as the day unfolded, there was precious little time to do anything but go with the flow. With the snow still pelting down, making it a magical Christmas Day, and the Christmas carol CD humming in the background, they cooked together and opened their presents. Pierre claimed that he loved the book and in return he gave her an antique clock, which she had seen on one of their trips together and had wistfully been tempted to buy but lacked the necessary funds.

'I *had* been hoping for a ring of some sort,' Didi said ruefully. 'One of those with a diamond somewhere.'

But then the moment was lost as the reality of turkey and mince pies and roast potatoes took over. By the time they sat to eat it was already after three, and as the snow stopped various of the neighbours dropped in for evening drinks.

Pierre, who usually abhorred these sorts of things, found himself rather enjoying it all. The previous years, bar one when he had been abroad on business, he had taken his mother out for Christmas lunch and they had enjoyed civilised, polite conversation in a variety of expensive restaurants or hotels.

But really, he now thought, this had been what she had truly wanted. Too much home-cooked food eaten with the pine smell of the Christmas tree mingling with the aroma of gravy and stuffing and far too many mince pies to be strictly healthy. She had wanted the neighbours over for drinks and village gossip and had probably warned them off in previous years suspecting that he would have hated it all.

In the corner of the room, Georgie was chatting vivaciously with the local vicar who, oddly, was wearing a Panama hat and looked ever so slightly like a member of the Mafia. Pierre caught her eye and raised his quickly skywards, up to the bedroom that awaited them, which made her blush madly and lose her thread of conversation.

He realised that he would return to his normal existence with a certain amount of regret. Understandable, he expected. Holidays for him were a rare occurrence and this one had certainly been out of the ordinary.

He glanced across to Georgie and as she met his eyes through the ten or so people gathered in the room, all talking animatedly about everything and nothing, Pierre's eyes narrowed and, like a man awakening from a dream, he saw what he should have seen some time ago.

For him, Georgie had first been a nuisance and then a novelty and finally a challenge and, while he had enjoyed every minute of her, he was sharp enough to know that he wanted his life to remain exactly how it was, uncluttered by emotion. He had kidded himself into thinking that she felt exactly the same way, but no. That expression on her face, which he now recognized, was not simply the complicit smile of a woman who wanted a man purely because they were good together in bed. That was the smile of a woman who was beginning to invest feelings in a relationship.

It wasn't going to do. Beyond the fact that he wasn't prepared for a committed relationship, he knew for certain that if he was, it wouldn't be with Georgie. Lovely and sweet as she was, she was also a country lass who could never make the leap into his world.

He felt a little shaken and quickly downed the remainder

of his drink and then he disappeared into his mother's study, which was crammed full of gardening books, recipe books and her favourite, crime thrillers. The desk was an old-fashioned one and naturally there was no computer, which was a modern gadget of which Didi heartily disapproved. 'Life worked perfectly well before they came along,' was her final word on the subject.

But it was perfectly adequate for thinking and Pierre didn't much care for the direction of his thoughts.

After twenty minutes, as he heard some of the opening and closing of the front door as the neighbours drifted off in pairs, he returned to the sitting room to find Georgie and his mother clearing away the various nibbles that had been brought out as fodder for the hungry masses.

'Bit of bad news, I'm afraid,' he said, interrupting the amicable chatter about nothing and everything. 'I'm going to have to leave first thing in the morning for Singapore.' Attuned that he now was to the reality of the situation, he noticed Georgie's expression, a mixture of disappointment and apprehension. Lord, but he would have to do something about that and sooner rather than later. 'Can't be helped,' he interrupted their protests and walked across to his mother and placed a kiss lightly on her head. 'I'll try and make it down for the new year, Didi, but I can't promise anything. Deals have no respect for holidays. I guess I should consider myself lucky that Singapore will only be for three days. Nothing worse than being on a plane on New Year's Eve. Somehow,' he tried to lighten the suddenly grey mood, 'party poppers and funny hats don't quite have the same fun quality.' Normally, Georgie would have laughed at this and cracked a joke about whether he would even recognise a party hat if it dropped onto his head, but she was silent and watchful.

Didi jumped into the awkward silence and began fussing

over him, asking concerned, rhetorical questions about whether he worked too hard and clucking in sympathy at the horror of having to work over the Christmas period, especially when they had all been having such a wonderful time.

Georgie didn't say a word and Pierre angrily read criticism in her wide green eyes. What had she been expecting? he wondered. A marriage proposal?

By the time Didi finally announced that she was heading upstairs and please don't forget to switch off the Christmas lights, old Mrs Evans had a terrible accident last Christmas with a burnt carpet, Pierre had latched onto a very healthy dose of anger and self-justification. What was Georgie *accusing him of* with those huge, reproachful eyes? Had he promised *anything*?

'I don't actually have to go anywhere,' he told her abruptly, shutting the kitchen door.

'Right.'

'But it's not, is it, Georgie?' He raked his fingers through his hair and Georgie looked back at him, not saying anything. Well, it had been going nowhere and nowhere had just come faster than she had expected. What on earth had she been thinking when she had imagined that she could somehow make herself indispensable? No one was indispensable to Pierre, possibly with the exception of his mother and that was what she now needed to focus on. The good things that had come out of their brief relationship. The good it had done for Didi, the good it had done for her relationship with her son.

'I thought we had a deal,' he told her accusingly. 'I thought we both knew the limits of…of *this*…'

'We do.'

'*I* do.' He walked across to the kitchen table and perched against it, staring at her. 'But this evening…this is real, Georgie, but it's something that exists purely in a moment in time. The truth is that I saw something on your face…you want more than I'm prepared to give…and, dammit, don't look at me like that!'

'Like what?' Pride warred with a desperate need to tell the truth. 'Okay. I know what you mean.' She sighed and lowered her eyes, staring at the quarry-tiled kitchen floor, which was a much safer area on which to focus her attention. 'I'm sorry I didn't obey the rules of the game, Pierre.' She laughed a little unsteadily. 'I don't know what came over me. One minute I really disapproved of you and everything you stood for and the next minute…' She shrugged. 'It happens. Our head says one thing and our heart still does crazy things.' Every word felt wrenched out of her but she kept her voice as neutral as she could. She could feel her heart doing crazy somersaults in her chest and all she could think was, *Why didn't I stop this when I could?*

'So you know why I think we have to call it a day.'

'No.' She looked at him directly in the eyes. 'No, I really don't. I'm not going to ask you to commit to anything, but why do you have to run scared just because I've got feelings for you and I've laid them on the line?'

'Run scared? *Run scared?* I can't believe what I'm hearing. I've never *run scared* of anything in my whole damned life, least of all a woman!'

'Then why don't you take a chance and go with this? I'm not asking you to give anything you don't feel capable of giving and I take full responsibility for looking after my own emotional welfare.' Her arms were tightly folded and she could feel her nails biting into her skin.

This was the first time anyone had ever suggested a direction in his life and he didn't like it. 'I'm not like you, Georgie,' he told her coolly. 'Taking a chance with a woman isn't in my brief. I have my working life and I have my emotional life and that's just the way it goes. I wasn't looking for a fairy-tale romance here when we slept together and nothing's changed. Besides...' and this to finally sever her from his life because he had been drifting these past few weeks and life was all about control, not aimless meandering down the high roads and byroads '—you're a nice girl but we don't live on the same planet.'

'I'm s small town girl and you're an uptown kind of guy, is that it?'

'To put it simply.' He frowned at her. 'You said it yourself more than once.'

'Okay.'

'And stop *saying okay*!'

'There's nothing more to say, Pierre. What will we say to Didi?'

'Leave it to me. I'll take care of it. You can surface when the dust has settled.'

'Right.'

'Don't waste your tears on me, Georgie. This is for the best. You move on with your life and I'll return to mine. Hopefully the next time we meet, this will all be history for you and there will be no awkwardness between us. After all, we've shared a lot these past couple of weeks.'

'Of course,' Georgie said politely. How very good to be concerned about her. He could counsel her on putting things behind her because he had no need to counsel himself. There was a hell of a lot to be said for being emotionally detached from the rest of the world. 'Time heals everything.' She turned around so that she could stare out of the kitchen window and, without looking over her shoulder, she said remotely, 'I'll leave tonight. That way you can explain things to Didi in the morning.'

Pierre opened his mouth, to say what he had no idea. In the end, he simply nodded at her erect back and quietly walked out of the kitchen.

CHAPTER TEN

MEETING his mother had been less than satisfactory. Pierre swivelled his chair and stared out of the glass panels of his office to a city finally surfacing from the stranglehold of winter. The trees were beginning to wake up and there was just the faintest tinge of warmth in the air, enough to encourage people to jettison their thick coats and stick on their macs.

He wondered what Georgia was wearing. How many of those hippie layers would she have stripped off to deal with the rise in temperature?

With a shake of his head, he dragged his thoughts back to Didi.

It had been her first visit to London for a very long time and Pierre had been irrationally thrilled by her obvious approval of his house. She had looked into every room, commenting on the colours and the pictures and declaring her approval as they had sat down for a cup of tea. Everything had been fine up to that point, then, fool that he was, he had angled the conversation round to Georgie.

There were still those regrets on his mother's side that things hadn't worked out between them, but in actual fact she had, three months previously when he had ruefully explained their split, accepted the situation with surprising calm.

Not wanting to dwell on the whole messy business for fear of opening a Pandora's box, Pierre had, at least to start with, made a determined effort not to mention Georgie when he spoke to Didi on the phone, which he now did at least twice a week. Gradually, though, his curiosity had got the better of him and he had begun dropping her name in the conversations, wondering how she was, angling for information because, as he told himself, he just wanted to make sure that she was okay, that she wasn't slipping into depression, and when Didi assured him that she was as right as rain he continued asking after her because, as he told his mother, she would have taken their break-up pretty hard and might well be putting on a front but going through personal agony. He just, he told her, didn't want Georgie falling over the edge.

So although he had told himself that Georgie's life was no longer his concern, he had still found himself asking his mother about her as they strolled through Harrods in search of a rug for his mother's sitting room, the old one having been finally put to rest.

And that was when the day had started to unravel because Georgie, his mother had said absent-mindedly as she had stroked one of the Persian rugs and debated whether it was worth the astronomical amount of money, was more than all right. She was seeing someone.

That was an eventuality Pierre hadn't expected and it had knocked him for six, but when he had casually suggested to his mother that it was probably a rebound relationship Didi had laughed out loud and informed him gaily that they seemed to be very serious indeed. He was, in her words, an absolutely charming man.

'A musician,' she confided, in between asking him for his opinion on three rugs she liked. Pierre pointed randomly to the nearest and then pressed her, as obliquely as he could, for details.

'What kind of musician?' He could hear the scorn in his voice and tempered it with polite interest. 'One of those long-haired types with body piercings, I expect. Maybe a tattoo on his arm somewhere?'

But no. A concert musician. No piercings, no tattoos, although apparently he did have lovely dark hair, which he raked back in a most attractive manner.

From that point on things, at least for Pierre, had gone from bad to worse. While his mother had merrily continued to enjoy the sights of London, he had battled with an increasingly foul temper.

And to even the score in his eyes, he had made the huge tactical error of inviting Sonya, a lawyer with whom he had worked a couple of times and who had slipped him her card with the explicit invitation for him to call *any time*, for dinner with them at a French restaurant in Chelsea.

It had not been a success. Sonya had tried too hard to impress by showing just how clever she was and Didi had been polite but distant. Several times Pierre had had to steer the conversation away from work-related issues that seemed numbingly tedious, but whichever direction he had turned Sonya had been determined to prove her worth. She had succeeded, he had thought afterwards, only in showing herself to be egotistical, insensitive and lacking in a sense of humour.

And now here he was. Didi was on her way back to Devon, probably napping in the back of the Bentley because his driver was taking her back. She had had a wonderful time. She had bought two rugs because choosing had been impossible, several spring outfits and little presents for Georgie, which Pierre had darkly imagined her sharing with her new musician boyfriend.

He stood up and glared down at the streets below. Three months! Three months and he was still wondering what she was up to! Except now, of course, he knew. She was showing someone else just what a talented little number she was between the sheets. And, more than that, probably planning all sorts of things together in the future. Engagements, weddings, two point two kids and the pet dog.

He dropped his head against the glass window and closed his eyes.

When he opened them he had made a decision. He wouldn't be able to take the Bentley but he wasn't averse to a spot of public transport. In fact, without having to concentrate on the roads, he would be able to think and he had a hell of a lot to think about, starting with why he had ever let her go and ending with whether he could win her back.

He left straight from his office. Like most aggressive men who felt uncomfortable with inactivity, Pierre was now filled with an urgency to see her. In fact, he would have taken the company helicopter but he couldn't be bothered with the arrangements and, besides, he really did need to decide what happened next and, worse, what he would do if she slammed the door in his face. A very real possibility considering how patronising he had been towards her at their last meeting.

Several hours later and the train deposited him into a steady drizzle for which he was ill prepared in his white shirt, tie and suit trousers minus the jacket, which might have protected him from the sudden bad weather.

Nerves, which had never been something from which he had suffered, suddenly kicked in and for a few seconds he contemplated turning round and heading back. But only for a few seconds. Then he shrugged off the thought and caught a taxi outside the station straight to her house.

The trip took under fifteen minutes. The joy of a traffic-free zone and he was deposited, in the gathering early evening twilight, right where he had a bird's eye view of the musician leaving her house. The musician with his dark hair and not a body piercing in sight. In fact very normal garb of pale trousers and a jumper underneath which he was wearing a collared shirt of some description. She didn't kiss him at the door but she might just as well have. The surge of jealous rage that ripped through Pierre was as savage as if they had made love in front of him.

He stuffed a wad of notes into the taxi driver's hand and stepped out of the taxi, slamming the door behind him, slamming it so loudly that he could see Georgie look across, startled.

Of course she didn't shut the door in his face, but he suspected that she might have been tempted to, and to spare them both from that particular temptation he bounded towards her, scowling as she pulled back ever so slightly, though when he was there, standing in front of her, her face was a mask of politeness.

'Hullo, Pierre. This is a surprise. How are you? Have you just dropped Didi off? I could have sworn she told me that she would be coming back with your driver.' If she had known that Pierre would be in the vicinity, she would have taken evasive action. The past months had been a nightmare and the last thing she needed was this, him standing in front of her for a courtesy visit, one of his 'we're adults, aren't we?' situations.

'Aren't you going to invite me in?' He gave her a twisted smile and placed one hand on the door, a semi-threatening gesture that she didn't fail to notice.

'I was just about to do some marking, actually, Pierre, so not a very good time…'

This time he stepped towards her. He was scaring her and that made him even angrier. Did she think that he would do something physical? Maybe she figured that he would try and force himself on her and naturally that thought would scare her, considering she had leapt into bed with another man in the space of seconds.

He tried to banish that thought but it crept into his head like poison.

'Now, now, that's not very sociable, is it?' He literally brushed past her into the hall, an immovable force now, and watched as she closed the door and leant against it. Barring the exit was just fine as far as he was concerned because he wasn't going anywhere. God he had missed her, missed her quirky ways, her laughter, her teasing, the way her hair looked as though it was waging a permanent war against restraint. She was wearing some faded jeans and a long-sleeved tee shirt and he had to shut his mind to the image of hands touching her under that tee shirt, pulling down those jeans.

'Would you like something to drink?' Georgie asked grudgingly. 'I could make you a quick cup of coffee.'

'Coffee would be...good.'

While she walked past him through to the kitchen, he looked around, searching for evidence of her new lover. He obviously hadn't as yet set up permanent camp in her house or else he wouldn't have been leaving, but that wasn't to say that he hadn't already begun the process of transferral.

'You'll have to be quick, Pierre. I haven't had much time today to work and I really need to get cracking.' Georgie stood politely by the kitchen door and waited.

'You know something, Georgie, forget the coffee. Just...tell me what you've been up to.' He folded his arms and leaned against the wall. 'Today.'

'I beg your pardon?'

'Today. What have you been up to *today*? No need to get all bowed down with details of the past three months.'

'Today...well...this and that...you know...the usual...' she stammered. 'You know...' If this was his idea of normal conversation, then why did it feel like a full-frontal attack?

And if she was beginning to piece her life back together, then why was her heart doing all sorts of desperate things? 'I want you to leave,' she said more forcefully, resenting the fact that he had virtually barged his way into her house and was now sabotaging all the hard work she had done trying to put her life back together.

'Why?' Pierre gritted. 'Expecting visitors? Or should I say *a visitor*?'

'I have no idea what you're talking about.'

'No?' he mocked, taking a couple of steps towards her. 'Don't give me that innocent expression, Georgie. Didi told me everything.'

'Didi told you everything?'

'That's right. The musician, apparently now the love of your life, and don't even try denying it. I saw him as he was leaving.' From a position of lifelong invulnerability, Pierre now realised that he would have to take the most terrifying leap of faith in his life. He loved her and he would have to sacrifice his pride and his self-control to tell her how he felt even though he felt, somewhere deep inside him, that it would all be for nothing. This, he was discovering, was what love did: it stripped a man of his defences and laid him bare to someone else's decisions.

'I...' He shook his head and glared at her. 'I...' He began again. 'I had to come here because I couldn't stand the thought of it, of another man in your life...'

This was a first, Georgie thought. She had seen all sides of this wonderful man with his complex personality, but never before had she seen him lost for words. And what on earth was he on about?

'Are you talking about Michael?'

'Whatever his name is.'

'What are you saying to me, Pierre? That you're *jealous*? I didn't think you *did* jealousy.'

'It would seem that I do.' He raked his fingers uncomfortably through his hair and met her eyes squarely.

'Tell me if I'm getting this right. You don't want me but you don't want anyone else to have me.'

'Partly true.' He would have to bare his soul and it felt like jumping off the edge of a precipice.

'Which part?'

'I don't want anyone else to even come near you, never mind *have you*. Having you is my right, Georgie, because... because I'm in love with you.' He watched as her mouth half opened and she went completely still and, before she could begin the horrific process of letting him down gently, he decided to tell her exactly how he felt and, once done, he would leave. It might scare the hell out of him but he wasn't going to back away having come this far. 'I thought what we had was just...fun. I didn't want complications in my life and I've always seen relationships as complications. I didn't want you falling in love with me because I figured my life had always worked just fine the way it had been before.'

'You're *in love with me*?'

'I've said my piece and I won't beg for you.' Or would he? He just didn't know and that was the humiliating thing. 'I...that guy...*you said you loved me*...' He looked away and then down at his feet. He could feel the muscles in his jaw clench.

'There's something I need to show you.' She stepped towards him and laid her hand gently on his arm. 'Come.' Her heart felt as if it were going to burst. The moment seemed as delicate as an eggshell.

She led him into the sitting room and pointed to the second-hand piano that was by the small bay window overlooking the back garden.

'The guy's brought his piano over? Is that what you want to show me?' Pierre asked bitterly.

'It's *my* piano,' Georgie said. 'Michael's my piano teacher. I thought it would be a nice thing to do and I needed something nice in my life after you left. I needed a distraction.'

'He's your *piano teacher*? Didi said...'

'Didi may have been a little naughty in her descriptions.' Georgie smiled and reached up to stroke the side of his face. 'How could you ever have imagined that I would see you walk out of my life and immediately get involved with someone else? I love you, Pierre.'

He took her hand in his and brought it to his lips, closing his eyes as he kissed her wrist and then let his mouth rest there for a while.

'I've missed you,' he said roughly. He led her to the sofa and pulled her down onto him so that he could properly feel her soft, yielding body against him. How could he ever have thought that he could live without this woman who had been fashioned to fit so perfectly with him? 'I haven't stopped thinking about you.' He held her face in both his hands and tenderly kissed her mouth. 'I thought I could live without you but it's been hell and, the worse it got, the more I told myself that I was doing the right thing. Then when Didi came...I felt as though I'd been kicked in the gut. Just the thought of you in someone else's arms...I felt physically sick.'

'And you came down.'

'I had to. For once in my life, I had absolutely no control over my actions. In fact, I don't think I've had much control over my actions since I met you, my darling. You took me out of my safe zone and I lost the desire to step back into it. Do you know I spent the entire train journey torn between needing to tell you how I felt and wanting to rip that musician man of yours to shreds.'

Georgie laughed. 'Michael would be horrified at that. Or maybe not horrified. Maybe amused. He's gay.'

'And Didi knew!'

'No. She just knew that I was seeing him for some piano lessons. She obviously decided to bend the basic truth for her nefarious purposes. And I'm glad she did or else you might never have taken that step to come down here.'

'I would have,' Pierre admitted heavily. 'My life was a mess. You were missing from it. I love you so much it hurts.' He slipped his hands under her tee shirt and cupping her breasts felt to him like coming home, back to the place he belonged. 'And I never want to go through the agony of not having you around. So. Will you marry me? For real?'

'Just try and stop me!'

Everything seemed so much easier than she could ever have anticipated. Didi was over the moon, naturally, and sheepishly admitted that perhaps she *had* exaggerated the truth about Michael *just a wee bit* to see if she might get the desired response.

The desired response was a small wedding at the local church six weeks later. Georgie wore a simple ivory silk dress and all the kids in her class were there, which made her want to burst into tears. She was leaving the school but would be back regularly to check on their progress, she warned them. But the fast life in London was not for her and neither, Pierre confessed, was it any longer for him. He had had a glimpse of how pleasurable life could be when lived at a slightly slower pace and so they had found a charming house in a village just outside Winchester. They would be able to visit Didi regularly and she would visit them.

Naturally, because it was Pierre, the process of house-hunting, which would have taken any normal person months, was accomplished in under two weeks. He *put his people onto it*, which meant that they sourced the possibilities, including some which were not technically possibilities but became so when large sums of money were waved in front of certain house owners. And so they simply had had to devote a couple of days to the business of looking around other people's homes.

Georgie laughingly told him that it was like being on one of those property shows on television where other people took the hard work out of house hunting.

But they had found the house of their dreams.

'You can even bring the chickens,' he told her as they looked round the huge garden with its forest of bluebells at the back. 'The kids will love playing with them.'

'*One child*,' Georgie corrected. Because that was something else. They had abandoned contraception and Nature had worked far more quickly than either of them had expected.

'So far.' Pierre looked at his new wife lovingly. Now a husband and, in only a few months, a father, and he was basking in the glory of it.

Children running through the sprawling old house, playing in the garden. He could imagine it all and when he looked at his beloved wife, he could tell that so could she.

And he was looking at her now as she stood at the little wooden railing smiling out to the moonlit sea, on their slightly delayed honeymoon to the most perfect island in the Indian Ocean.

He wrapped his arms around her and she leaned back into him and sighed.

'You're beginning to show,' he murmured. 'Sexy.'

Georgie laughed and swung round so that she was facing him. 'What are you trying to say?' she asked, grinning.

'That I predict the view will be a lot more tempting in an hour's time? After I've shown you just how sexy I think my pregnant woman is...' He slipped his hand under her loose cotton top. No bra. Just how he liked it. Her soft breasts fitted perfectly in his big hands and he gently caressed them until her eyelids were fluttering, her head thrown back as she relished what he was doing to her. 'Tempted at all, my darling?'

Georgie tiptoed and kissed him, then she slowly nodded. He was right. The scenery could wait for later. Right now she wanted him touching her, suckling on her nipples, which were already getting bigger and darker, teasing between her legs with his fingers and his mouth.

Paradise wasn't just the stunning scenery and the crystal-blue water and the powdery sand. Paradise was wherever he was and always would be.

* * * * *

The debt, the payment, the price!

A ruthless ruler and his virgin queen. Trembling with the fragility of new spring buds, Ionanthe will go to her husband. She was given as penance, but he'll take her for pleasure!

Harlequin Presents® is delighted to unveil an exclusive extract from Penny Jordan's new book
A BRIDE FOR HIS MAJESTY'S PLEASURE

PEOPLE WERE PRESSING in on her—the crowd was carrying her along with it, almost causing her to lose her balance. Fear stabbed through Ionanthe as she realized how vulnerable she was.

An elderly man grabbed her arm, warning her, 'You had better do better by our prince than that sister of yours. She shamed us all when she shamed him.'

Spittle flecked his lips, and his eyes were wild with anger as he shook her arm painfully. The people surrounding her who had been smiling before were now starting to frown, their mood changing. She looked around for the guards, but couldn't see any of them. She was alone in a crowd that was quickly becoming hostile to her. She hadn't thought it was in her nature to panic, but she was beginning to do so now.

Then Ionanthe felt another hand on her arm, in a touch that extraordinarily her body somehow recognized. And a familiar voice was saying firmly, 'Princess Ionanthe has already paid the debt owed by her family to the people of Fortenegro. Her presence here today as my bride and your princess is proof of that.'

He was at her side now, his presence calming the crowd and forcing the old man to release her as the crowd began to murmur their agreement to his words.

Calmly but determinedly Max was guiding her back through the crowd. A male voice called out to him from the crowd. 'Make sure you get us a fine future prince on her as soon as may be, Your Highness.'

The sentiment was quickly taken up by others, who threw in their own words of bawdy advice to the new bridegroom. Ionanthe fought to stop her face from burning with angry humiliated color. Torn between unwanted relief that she had been rescued and discomfort about what was being said, Ionanthe took refuge in silence as they made their way back toward the palace.

They had almost reached the main entrance when once again Max told hold of her arm. This time she fought her body's treacherous reaction, clamping down on the sensation that shot through her veins and stiffening herself against it. The comments she had been subjected to had brought home to her the reality of what she had done; they clung inside her head, rubbing as abrasively against her mind as burrs would have rubbed against her skin.

'Isn't it enough for you to have forced me into marrying you? Must you force me to obey your will physically, as well?' she challenged him bitterly.

Max felt the forceful surge of his own anger swelling through him to meet her biting contempt, shocking him with its intensity as he fought to subdue it.

Not once during the months he had been married to Eloise had she ever come anywhere near arousing him emotionally the way that Ionanthe could, despite the fact that he had known her only a matter of days. She seemed to delight in pushing him—punishing him for their current situation, no doubt, he reminded himself as his anger subsided. It was completely out of character for him to let anyone get under his skin enough to make him react emotionally when his response should be purely cerebral.

'Far from wishing to force you to do anything, I merely wanted to suggest that we use the side entrance to the palace. That way we will attract less attention.'

He had a point, Ionanthe admitted grudgingly, but she wasn't going to say so. Instead she started to walk toward the door set in one of the original castle towers, both of them slipping through the shadows the building now threw across the square, hidden from the view of the people crowding the palace steps. She welcomed the peace of its stone interior after the busyness of the square. Her dress had become uncomfortably heavy and her head had started to ache. The reality of what she had done had begun to set in, filling her with a mixture of despair and panic. But she mustn't think of herself and her immediate future, she told herself as she started to climb the stone steps that she knew from memory led to a corridor that connected the old castle to the more modern palace.

She had almost reached the last step when somehow or other she stepped on the hem of her gown, the accidental movement unbalancing her and causing her to stumble. Max, who was several steps below her, heard the small startled sound she made and raced up the stairs, catching her as she fell.

If she was trembling with the fragility of new spring buds in the wind, then it was because of her shock. If she felt weak and her heart was pounding with dangerous speed, then it was because of the weight of her gown. If she couldn't move, then it was because of the arms that imprisoned her.

She had to make him release her. It was dangerous to be in his arms. She looked up at him, her gaze traveling the distance from his chin to his mouth and then refusing to move any farther. What had been a mere tremor of shock had now become a fiercely violent shudder that came from deep within her and ached through her. She felt dizzy, light-headed, removed from everything about herself she considered 'normal' to become, instead, a woman who hungered for something unknown and forbidden.

* * * * *

Give yourself a present this Christmas—
pick up a copy of
A BRIDE FOR HIS MAJESTY'S PLEASURE
by Penny Jordan,
available December 2009 from Harlequin Presents®!

INNOCENT WIVES

Powerful men—ready to wed!

They're passionate, persuasive and don't
play by the rules...they make them!

And now they need brides.

But when their innocent wives say "I Do," can it ever
be more than a marriage in name only?

Look out for all our exciting books this month:

Powerful Greek, Unworldly Wife #81
by SARAH MORGAN

Ruthlessly Bedded, Forcibly Wedded #82
by ABBY GREEN

Blackmailed Bride, Inexperienced Wife #83
by ANNIE WEST

The British Billionaire's Innocent Bride #84
by SUSANNE JAMES

HPE1209

REQUEST YOUR FREE BOOKS!

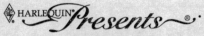 HARLEQUIN *Presents*

2 FREE NOVELS PLUS 2 FREE GIFTS!

YES! Please send me 2 FREE Harlequin Presents® novels and my 2 FREE gifts (gifts are worth about $10). After receiving them, if I don't wish to receive any more books, I can return the shipping statement marked "cancel". If I don't cancel, I will receive 6 brand-new novels every month and be billed just $4.05 per book in the U.S. or $4.74 per book in Canada. That's a savings of close to 15% off the cover price! It's quite a bargain! Shipping and handling is just 50¢ per book*. I understand that accepting the 2 free books and gifts places me under no obligation to buy anything. I can always return a shipment and cancel at any time. Even if I never buy another book, the two free books and gifts are mine to keep forever.

106 HDN EYRQ   306 HDN EYR2

Name	(PLEASE PRINT)

Address		Apt. #

City	State/Prov.	Zip/Postal Code

Signature (if under 18, a parent or guardian must sign)

Mail to the Harlequin Reader Service:
IN U.S.A.: P.O. Box 1867, Buffalo, NY 14240-1867
IN CANADA: P.O. Box 609, Fort Erie, Ontario L2A 5X3

Not valid to current subscribers of Harlequin Presents books.

Are you a current subscriber of Harlequin Presents books and want to receive the larger-print edition? Call 1-800-873-8635 today!

* Terms and prices subject to change without notice. Prices do not include applicable taxes. Sales tax applicable in N.Y. Canadian residents will be charged applicable provincial taxes and GST. Offer not valid in Quebec. This offer is limited to one order per household. All orders subject to approval. Credit or debit balances in a customer's account(s) may be offset by any other outstanding balance owed by or to the customer. Please allow 4 to 6 weeks for delivery. Offer available while quantities last.

Your Privacy: Harlequin Books is committed to protecting your privacy. Our Privacy Policy is available online at www.eHarlequin.com or upon request from the Reader Service. From time to time we make our lists of customers available to reputable third parties who may have a product or service of interest to you. If you would prefer we not share your name and address, please check here. ☐

HP09R

HARLEQUIN *Presents*

TWO CROWNS, TWO ISLANDS, ONE LEGACY

A royal family torn apart by pride and its lust for power, reunited by purity and passion

THE ROYAL HOUSE *of* KAREDES

Harlequin Presents is proud to bring you
the last three installments from
The Royal House of Karedes.
You won't want to miss out!

THE FUTURE KING'S LOVE-CHILD
by Melanie Milburne, December 2009

RUTHLESS BOSS, ROYAL MISTRESS
by Natalie Anderson, January 2010

THE DESERT KING'S HOUSEKEEPER BRIDE
by Carol Marinelli, February 2010

Darkly handsome—proud and arrogant
The perfect Sicilian husbands!

DANTE: CLAIMING HIS SECRET LOVE-CHILD

by

Sandra Marton

The patriarch of a powerful Sicilian dynasty,
Cesare Orsini, has fallen ill, and he wants atonement
before he dies. One by one he sends for his sons—
he has a mission for each to help him clear his
conscience. His sons are proud and determined,
but the tasks they undertake will change
their lives forever!

Book #2877

Available November 24, 2009

Look for the next installment
from Sandra Marton coming in 2010!